GW01417928

Household Masonic Library.

THE

CONSTITUTIONS

OF THE

FREE-MASONS;

CONTAINING THE

History, Charges and Regulations

OF THAT MOST

ANCIENT AND RIGHT WORSHIPFUL FRATERNITY.

FOR THE USE OF THE LODGES.

LONDON:

Printed by WM. HUNTER, for JOHN SENEX, at the *Globe*, and JOHN HOOKE at the *Flower-de-Luce*, over-against *St. Dunstan's Church*, in Fleet st.

In the Year of Masonry, 5723 — Anno Domini, 1723.

NEW YORK:

ROBT. MACOY, 29 BEEKMAN STREET.

CLARK, AUSTIN & SMITH, 3 PARK ROW.

1859.

HS 440
A6
1859

AMERICAN PUBLISHER'S PREFACE.

THE year 1723 forms an important epoch in the history of the Order, and among the Masonic writers of that period there are few more deserving of notice than the author of the "Constitutions of Freemasonry." The Masonic world have already dignified him with the reputation of a classic, and enrolled his name among that select number whose works belong alike to every nation, and are destined to float down the stream of time, untouched by the flood of oblivion, which soon overtakes the mass of authors, as it does the mass of other men.

"*Incredibili industriæ* — diligentia singulari," said the ancients in their descriptions of individuals eminent for merit; and, indeed, it must be owned that, in his laborious compilations, "extracted from the ancient records of lodges beyond sea"—a work characterized by industry and the love of truth—no writer is more eminently entitled to the encomium than JAMES ANDERSON. His varied acquirements, deep research, wonderful industry, great experience and boundless resources of knowledge, both practical and theoretical, have done much to advance the cause of Masonry.

M510949

Dr. ANDERSON's work made its appearance at a most seasonable time; for he himself says, " It is highly probable that many valuable documents relative to the Society were destroyed, at the revival of the Order in 1717." No pains were spared—no labor lost—in examining the old records for Masonic information· Six years afterwards the work which has done so much honor to its author, appeared as a vehicle of valuable intelligence to the craft, and without which no Masonic library is now complete.

In presenting an American edition of "Anderson's Constitutions" to the Masonic Fraternity, the Publisher feels confident that there are but few readers in the Order who have not dwelt with interest and delight on the pages of this most popular work—popular at least with Masons, and esteemed by them as the *written* Landmarks of Masonry.

'The orthography of the original London edition of 1723, of which this work is a reprint, is scrupulously followed and retained. The typographical execution of the present edition will render it, no doubt, an ornament to the library, so that by this means the Publisher is able to include in a *neat, economical* and *substantial form,* a large amount of instruction on the most important principles of the Order.

DEDICATION.

TO

HIS GRACE THE DUKE OF MONTAGU.

MY LORD,

BY Order of his GRACE the DUKE OF WHARTON, the present Right Worshipful GRAND MASTER of the FREE-MASONS ; and, as his Deputy, I humbly dedicate this BOOK OF THE CONSTITUTIONS of our ancient FRATERNITY to your GRACE, in testimony of your honourable, prudent, and vigilant discharge of the office of our GRAND-MA-TER last year.

I need not tell your GRACE what pains our learned AUTHOR has taken in compiling and digesting this book from the OLD RECORDS, and how accurately he has compared and made every thing agreeable to HISTORY and CHRONOLOGY, so as to render these NEW CONSTITUTIONS a just and exact account of MASONRY from the beginning of the World to your GRACE'S MASTERSHIP, still preserv-

1*

ing all that was truly ancient and authentick in the old ones : For every Brother will be pleased with the performance, that knows it had your GRACE's perusal and approbation, and that it is now printed for the use of the LODGES, after it was approved by the GRAND-LODGE, when your GRACE was GRAND MASTER. All the BROTHERHOOD will ever remember the honour your GRACE has done them, and your care for their Peace, Harmony, and lasting Friendship : Which none is more duly sensible of than,

   My LORD,

    Your GRACE's

     Most oblig'd, and

      Most obedient Servant,

       And Faithful Brother,

        J. T. DESAGULIERS,

        Deputy Grand-Master.

THE

CONSTITUTION,

HISTORY, LAWS, CHARGES, ORDERS, REGULATIONS,
AND USAGES,

OF THE RIGHT WORSHIPFUL FRATERNITY OF

ACCEPTED FREE MASONS;

COLLECTED

𝔉rom their General Records, and the faithful
Traditions of many Ages.

TO BE READ

At the Admission of a NEW BROTHER, when the MASTER
or WARDEN shall begin, or order some other Brother
to read as follows :

ADAM, our first parent, created after the image of GOD, the great Architect of the Universe, must have had the Liberal Sciences, particularly GEOMETRY, written on his heart; for, even since the fall we find the principles of it in the hearts of his offspring, and which, in process of time, have been drawn forth into a convenient method of propositions, by observing the LAWS of PROPORTION, taken from Mechanism ; so that, as the Mechanical Arts gave occasion to the learned to reduce the elements of Geometry into method, this noble science, thus reduced, is the foundation of all those arts, (particularly of MA-

SONRY and ARCHITECTURE) and the rule by which they are conducted and performed.

No doubt ADAM taught his sons Geometry, and the use of it, in the several arts and crafts convenient, at least, for those early times ; for CAIN, we find, built a city, which he called Consecrated, or Dedicated, after the name of his eldest son ENOCH ; and becoming the Prince of the one half of mankind, his posterity would imitate his royal example in improving both the noble science and the useful art.*

Nor can we suppose that SETH was less instructed, who, being the Prince of the other half of mankind, and also the prime cultivator of Astronomy, would take equal care to teach Geometry and Masonry to his offspring, who had also the mighty advantage of ADAM's living among them.†

But without regarding uncertain accounts, we may safely conclude the Old World, that lasted

* As other Arts were also improved by them, viz: working in metal by TUBAL CAIN, music by JUBAL, pasturage and tent-making by JABAL, which last is good architecture.

† For by some vestiges of antiquity we find one of 'em, godly ENOCH, (who dy'd not, but was translated alive to Heaven) prophecying of the final conflagration AT THE DAY OF JUDGMENT (as St. JUDE tells us) and likewise of the general Deluge for the punishment of the world : Upon which he erected his two large pillars, (tho' some ascribe them to Seth) the one of stone, and the other of brick, whereon were engraven the Liberal Sciences, &c. And that the stone pillar remain'd in Syria until the days of VESPASIAN the Emperor.

1,656 years, could not be ignorant of Masonry; and that both the families of SETH and CAIN erected many curious works, until at length NOAH, the ninth from SETH, was commanded and directed of God to build the great Ark, which, though of wood, was certainly fabricated by Geometry, and according to the rules of Masonry.

NOAH, and his three sons, JAPHET, SHEM, and HAM, all Masons true, brought with them over the flood the traditions and arts of the antedeluvians, and amply communicated them to their growing off-spring; for about 101 years after the flood, we find a vast number of them, if not the whole race of NOAH, in the vale of Shinar, employed in building a city and large tower, in order to make to themselves a name, and to prevent their dispersion. And though they carried on the work to a monstrous height, and by their vanity provoked God to confound their devices, by confounding their speech, which occasioned their dispersion, yet their skill in Masonry is not the less to be celebrated, having spent above 53 years in that prodigious work, and upon their dispersion carried the mighty knowledge with them into distant parts, where they found the good use of it in the settlement of their kingdoms, commonwealths, and dynasties. And though afterwards it was lost in most parts of the earth, it was especially preserved in Shinar and Assyria, where

NIMROD,* the founder of that monarchy, after the dispersion, built many splendid cities, as Ereck, Accad, and Calneh, in Shinar ; from whence afterwards he went forth into Assyria, and built Nini-veh, Rehoboth, Caleh, and Rhesin.

In these parts, upon the Tygris and Euphrates, afterwards flourished many learned priests and ma-thematicians, known by the names of Chaldees and Magi, who preserved the good science Geometry, as the kings and great men encouraged the Royal Art. But it is not expedient to speak more plain of the premises, except in a formed Lodge.

From hence, therefore, the Science and Art were both transmitted to latter ages and distant climes, notwithstanding the confusion of languages or dia-lects, which, though it might help to give rise to the Masons' faculty and ancient universal practice of conversing without speaking, and of knowing each other at a distance, yet hindered not the improve-ment of Masonry in each colony, and their communi-cation in their distinct national dialect.

And no doubt the Royal Art was brought down to Egypt by MITZRAIM, the second son of HAM, about six years after the confusion at Babel, and

* NIMROD, which signifies a REBEL, was the name given him by the holy Family, and by MOSES ; but among his friends in CHAL-DEA, his proper name was BELUS, which signifies LORD ; and afterwards was worshipped as a God by many nations, under the name of BEL, or BAAL, and became the BACCHUS of the Ancients, or BAR CHUS, the son of CHUS.

after the flood 160 years, when he led thither his colony; (for Egypt is MITZRAIM in Hebrew) because we find the river Nile's overflowing its banks soon caused an improvement in Geometry, which consequently brought Masonry much in request; for the ancient noble cities, with the other magnificent edifices of that country, and particularly the famous Pyramids, demonstrate the early taste and genius of that ancient kingdom. Nay, one of those Egyptian Pyramids* is reckoned the first of the seven wonders of the world, the account of which, by historians and travellers, is almost incredible.

The Sacred Records inform us well that the eleven great sons of CANAAN (the youngest son of HAM) soon fortified themselves in strongholds and stately walled cities, and erected most beautiful temples and mansions; for, when the Israelites, under the great JOSHUA, invaded their country, they found it so regularly fenced, that without the immediate intervention of God in behalf of his peculiar people, the Canaanites were impregnable and invincible. Nor can we suppose less of the other sons of HAM, viz: CHUSH, his eldest, in South Arabia,

---

° The marble stones, brought a vast way from the quarries of ARABIA, were most of 'em 80 foot long; and its foundation cover'd the ground of 700 foot on each side, or 2800 foot in compass, and 481 in perpendicular height. And in perfecting it were employ'd every day, for 20 whole years, 360,000 men, by some ancient EGYPTIAN KING, long before the ISRAELITES were a people, for the honor of his Empire, and at last to become his TOMB.

and PHUT, or PHUTS, (now called FEZ) in West
Africa.

And surely the fair and gallant posterity of
JAPHET, (the eldest son of NOAH) even such as
travelled into the isles of the Gentiles, must have
been equally skilled in Geometry and Masonry;
though we know little of their transactions and
mighty works until their original knowledge was
almost lost by the havock of war, and by not maintaining a due correspondence with the polite and
learned nations; for, when that correspondence was
opened in after ages, we find they began to be most
curious architects.

The posterity of SHEM had also equal opportuni-
ties of cultivating the useful art, even those of them
that planted their colonies in the south and east of
Asia, much more those of them that in the great
Assyrian empire lived in a separate state, or were
blended with other families: nay, that holy branch
of SHEM (of whom, as concerning the flesh, Christ
came) could not be unskilful in the learned arts of
Assyria; for ABRAM, after the confusion at Babel
about 268 years, was called out of Ur of the Chaldees, where he learned Geometry, and the arts that
are performed by it, which he would carefully trans-
mit to ISHMAEL, to ISAAC, and to his sons, by KETU-
RAH; and by ISAAC, to ESAU and JACOB, and the
twelve Patriarchs; nay, the Jews believe that

ABRAM also instructed the Egyptians in the Assyrian learning.

Indeed, the select family long used military architecture only, as they were sojourners among strangers ; but before the 430 years of their peregrination were expired, even about 86 years before their exodus, the Kings of Egypt forced most of them to lay down their shepherd's instruments and warlike accoutrements, and trained them to another sort of architecture in stone and brick, as Holy Writ and other histories acquaint us, which GOD did wisely over-rule, in order to make them good Masons before they possessed the promised land, then famous for most curious Masonry.

And while marching to Canaan, through Arabia, under MOSES, God was pleased to inspire BEZALEEL, of the tribe of Judah, and AHOLIAB, of the tribe of Dan, with wisdom of heart for erecting that most glorious tent or tabernacle, wherein the Shechinah resided, which, though not of stone or brick, was framed by Geometry, a most beautiful piece of architecture, (and proved afterwards the model of SOLOMON'S Temple) according to the pattern that GOD had shown to MOSES in the Mount ; who therefore became the General Master Mason, as well as King of Jessurun, being well skilled in all the Egyptian learning, and divinely inspired with more sublime knowledge in Masonry.

So that the Israelites, at their leaving Egypt, were

a whole kingdom of Masons, well instructed, under the conduct of their Grand Master MOSES, who often marshalled them into a regular and general Lodge, while in the wilderness, and gave them wise charges, orders, &c., had they been well observed! But no more of the premises must be mentioned.

And after they were possessed of Canaan, the Israelites came not short of the old inhabitants in Masonry, but rather vastly improved it, by the special direction of Heaven; they fortified better, and improved their city houses and the palaces of their chiefs, and only fell short in sacred architecture while the Tabernacle stood, but no longer; for the finest sacred building of the Canaanites was the Temple of Dagon in Gaza of the Philistines, very magnificent, and capacious enough to receive 5000 people under its roof, that was artfully supported by two main columns,* and was a wonderful discovery of their mighty skill in true Masonry, as must be owned.

But Dagon's Temple, and the finest structures of Tyre and Sidon, could not be compared with the Eternal GOD's Temple at Jerusalem, begun and

---

* By which the glorious SAMPSON pull'd it down upon the Lords of the PHILISTINES, and was also entangled in the same death which he drew upon his enemies for putting out his eyes, after he had reveal'd his secrets to his wife, that betray'd him into their hands; for which weakness he never had the honor to be numbered among Masons: But it is not convenient to write more of this.

finished, to the amazement of all the world, in the
short space of seven years and six months, by that
wisest man and most glorious King of Israel, the
Prince of Peace and Architecture, SOLOMON, (the
son of DAVID, who was refused that honour for
being a man of blood) by divine direction, without
the noise of workmen's tools, though there were employed about it no less than 3,600 Princes,* or
Master Masons, to conduct the work according to
SOLOMON's directions, with 80,000 hewers of stone
in the mountain, or Fellow Craftsmen, and 70,000
labourers, in all .　.　.　.　.　153,600
Besides the levy under ADONIRAM to
　work in the mountains of Lebanon by
　turns with the Sidonians, viz : .　.　30,000

being in all .　.　.　.　.　.　183,600

* In I KINGS, v. 16, they are call'd חורדים HARODIM, Rulers or
Provosts assisting King SOLOMON, who were set over the work,
and their number there is only 3,300: But 2 CHRON. II. 18, they
are called מנצהים MENATZCHIM, Overseers and Comforters of the
people in working, and in number, 3,600; because either 300
might be more curious artists, and the OVERSEERS of the said
3,300, or rather, not so excellent, and only DEPUTY-MASTERS, to
supply their places in case of death or absence, that so there
might be always 3,300 ACTING MASTERS compleat; or else they
might be the OVERSEERS of the 70,000 סבל איש ISH SABBAL, men
of burden, or labourers, who were not Masons, but served the
80,000 הצב איש ISH CHOTZEB, men of Hewing, called also גבלים
GHIBLIM, stone-cutters and sculpturers; and also, BONAI, בני
Builders in stone, part of which belonged to SOLOMON, and part
to HIRAM, King of TYRE, I KINGS, v. 18.

for which great number of ingenious Masons, Solomon was much obliged to Hiram, or Huram, King
of Tyre, who sent his masons and carpenters to
Jerusalem, and the firs and cedars of Lebanon to
Joppa, the next sea-port.

But above all, he sent his namesake Hiram, or
Huram, the most accomplished Mason upon earth.*

And the prodigious expence of it also enhaunceth
its excellency ; for besides King David's vast pre-
parations, his richer son Solomon, and all the

---

* We read (2 Chron. ii. 13.) Hiram, King of Tyre, (called there
Huram) in his letter to King Solomon, says, I have sent a
cunning Man, להורם אבי le Huram Abhi, not to be translated
according to the vulgar Greek and Latin, Huram my Father, as
if this Architect was King Hiram's Father; for his description,
ver. 14, refutes it, and the original plainly imports, Huram of
my Father's, viz. the chief Master-Mason of my Father, King
Abibulus; (who enlarg'd and beautify'd the city of Tyre, as
ancient histories inform us, whereby the Tyrians at this time
were most expert in Masonry) tho' some think Hiram the King
might call Hiram the Architect Father, as learned and skillful
men were wont to be call'd of old times, or as Joseph was call'd
the Father of Pharaoh ; and as the same Hiram is call'd Solomon's Father, (2 Chron. iv. 16.) where 'tis said

שלמה   למלך   אביר   חורם   עשה
Shelomoh   lammelech   Abhif   Churam   ghnasah,
Did Huram, his Father, make to King Solomon.

But the difficulty is over at once, by allowing the word Abif
to be the surname of Hiram the Mason, called also (Chap. ii. 13.)
Hiram Abi, as here Hiram Abif; for being so amply describ'd,
(Chap. ii. 14.) we may easily suppose his surname would not be
conceal'd : And this reading makes the sense plain and compleat,
viz. that Hiram, King of Tyre, sent to King Solomon his namesake Hiram Abif, the Prince of Architects, describ'd (1 Kings, vii.

wealthy Israelites, and the nobles of all the neighbouring kingdoms, largely contributed towards it
in gold, silver, and rich jewels, that amounted to a
sum almost incredible.

Nor do we read of anything in Canaan so large,
the wall that inclosed it being 7,700 foot in compass; far less any holy structure fit to be named
with it, for exactly proportioned and beautiful di-
mensions, from the magnificent porch on the east to

14.) to be a Widow's Son of the Tribe of Napthali; and in (2
Chron. ii. 14.) the said King of Tyre calls him the son of a woman
of the daughters of DAN; and in both places, that his father was
a man of Tyre; which difficulty is remov'd, by supposing his
Mother was either of the Tribe of DAN, or of the Daughters of
the city call'd DAN in the Tribe of NAPTHALI, and his deceased
Father had been a NAPTHALITE, whence his Mother was call'd a
widow of Napthali; for his Father is not call'd a Tyrian by
descent, but a man of Tyre by habitation; as OBED EDOM the Levite
is call'd a Gittite by living among the Gittites, and the Apostle
PAUL a man of Tarsus. But supposing a mistake in transcribers,
and that his Father was really a Tyrian by blood, and his Mother
only of the Tribe of DAN or NAPTHALI, that can be no bar
against allowing of his vast capacity; for as his Father was a
worker in brass, so he himself was fill'd with wisdom and understanding, and cunning to work all works in brass: And as King
SOLOMON sent for him, so King HIRAM, in his letter to SOLOMON,
says, And now I have sent a cunning man, endued with understanding, skilful to work in gold, silver, brass, iron, stone,
timber, purple, blue, fine linnen and crimson; also to grave any
manner of graving, and to find out every device which shall be
put to him, with thy cunning men, and with the cunning men
of my Lord DAVID thy Father. This divinely inspired workman
maintain'd this character in erecting the Temple, and in working
the utensils thereof, far beyond the performances of AHOLIAB and
BEZALEEL, being also universally capable of all sorts of Masonry.

the glorious and reverend Sanctum Sanctorum on
the west, with most lovely and convenient apartments for the Kings and Princes, Priests and Le-
vites, Israelites, and Gentiles also ; it being an
House of Prayer for all nations, and capable of receiving in the Temple proper, and in all its courts
and apartments together, no less than 300,000
people, by a modest calculation, allowing a square
cubit to each person.

And if we consider the 1,453 columns of Parian
marble, with twice as many Pillasters, both having
glorious capitals of several orders, and about 2,246
windows, besides those in the pavement, with the
unspeakable and costly decorations of it within;
(and much more might be said) we must conclude
its prospect to transcend our imagination ; and that
it was justly esteemed by far the finest piece of
Masonry upon earth before or since, and the chief
wonder of the world ; and was dedicated or consecrated, in the most solemn manner, by King
SOLOMON.

But leaving what must not, and indeed cannot
be communicated by writing, we may warrantably
affirm, that however ambitious the heathen were in
cultivating of the Royal Art, it was never perfected
until GOD condescended to instruct his peculiar
people in rearing the above-mentioned stately tent,
and in building at length this gorgeous house, fit
for the special refulgence of his glory, where he

dwelt between the Cherubims on the Mercy-Seat, and from thence gave them frequent oraculous responses.

This most sumptuous, splendid, beautiful, and glorious edifice, attracted soon the inquisitive artists of all nations to spend some time at Jerusalem, and survey its peculiar excellencies, as much as was allowed to the Gentiles, whereby they soon discovered that all the world, with their joint skill, came far short of the Israelites in the wisdom and dexterity of architecture, when the wise King SOLOMON was Grand Master of the Lodge at Jerusalem, and the learned King HIRAM was Grand Master of the Lodge at Tyre, and the inspired HIRAM ABIF was Master of Work, and Masonry was under the immediate care and direction of Heaven, when the noble and the wise thought it their honour to be assisting to the ingenious Masters and Craftsmen, and when the Temple of the true GOD became the wonder of all travellers, by which, as by the most perfect pattern, they corrected the architecture of their own country upon their return.

So that after the erection of SOLOMON's Temple, Masonry was improved in all the neighbouring nations; for the many artists employed about it, under HIRAM ABIF, after it was finished, dispersed themselves into Syria, Mesopotamia, Assyria, Chaldea, Babylonia, Media, Persia, Arabia, Africa, Lesser Asia, Greece, and other parts of Europe, where they

taught this liberal art to the free born sons of eminent persons, by whose dexterity the kings, princes,
and potentates built many glorious piles, and became the Grand Masters, each in his own territory,
and were emulous of excelling in this Royal Art ;
nay, even in India, where the correspondence was
open, we may conclude the same ; but none of the
nations, nor all together, could rival the Israelites,
far less excel them, in Masonry, and their Temple
remained the constant pattern.*

Nay, the Grand Monarch NEBUCHADNEZAR could
never, with all his unspeakable advantages, carry up
his Masonry to the beautiful strength and magnificence of the Temple work, which he had, in warlike
rage, burnt down, after it had remained in splendor

---

* For tho' the Temple of Diana at Ephesus is suppos'd to have
been first built by some of JAPHET's posterity, that made a settlement in Jonia about the time of MOSES; yet it was often demol-
ish'd, and then rebuilt for the sake of improvements in Masonry ;
and we cannot compute the period of its last glorious erection
(that became another of the seven wonders of the world) to be
prior to that of SOLOMON's Temple ; but that long afterwards the
Kings of Lesser Asia join'd, for 220 years, in finishing it, with
107 columns of the finest marble, and many of them with most
exquisite sculpture (each at the expence of a King, by the Master-
Mason's DRESIPHON and ARCHIPHRON) to support the planked
cieling and roof of pure cedar, as the doors and linings were of
cypress : Whereby it became the mistress of Lesser Asia, in length
425 foot, and in breadth 220 foot : Nay, so admirable a fabrick,
that XERXES left it standing when he burnt all the other temples
in his way to Greece ; tho' at last it was set on fire and burnt
down by a vile fellow, only for the lust of being talk'd of, on
the very day that ALEXANDER the GREAT was born.

416 years from its consecration. For after his wars
were over, and general peace proclaimed, he set his
heart on architecture, and became the Grand Master Mason ; and having before led captive the
ingenious artists of Judea, and other conquered
countries, he raised indeed the largest work upon
earth, even the walls* and city, the palaces and
hanging gardens, the bridge and temple of Babylon,
the third of the seven wonders of the world, though

* In thickness, 87 foot, in height 350 foot, and in compass 480
furlongs, or 60 British miles in an exact square of 15 miles a side,
built of large bricks, cemented with the hard bitumen of that
old vale of Shinar, with 100 gates of brass, or 25 a-side, and 250
towers ten foot higher than the wall.

From the said 25 gates in each side went 25 streets in strait
lines, or in all 50 streets, each 15 miles long, with four half
streets next the walls, each 200 foot broad, as the entire streets
were 150 foot broad : And so the whole city was thus cut out into
676 squares, each being 2 miles and ¼ in compass ; round which
were the houses built three or four stories high, well-adorn'd,
and accommodated with yards, gardens, &c. A branch of the
Euphrates run thro' the middle of it, from north to south, over
which, in the heart of the city, was built a stately bridge, in
length a furlong, and thirty foot in breadth, by wonderful art,
for supplying the want of a foundation in the river. At the two
ends of this bridge were two magnificent palaces, the old palace,
the seat of ancient Kings, at the east end, upon the ground of
four squares : and the new palace at the west end, built by NEB-
UCHADNEZZAR, upon the ground of nine squares, with hanging-
gardens (so much celebrated by the Greeks) where the loftiest
trees could grow as in the fields, erected in a square of 400 foot,
on each side, carried up by terraces, and sustained by vast arches
built upon arches, until the highest terrace equal'd the height
of the city-walls, with a curious aqueduct to water the whole
gardens. Old Babel improv'd, stood on the east side of the river,

2

vastly inferior, in the sublime perfection of Masonry,
to the holy, charming, lovely Temple of GOD. But
as the Jewish captives were of special use to NEBU-
CHADNEZZAR in his glorious buildings, so being thus
kept at work, they retained their great skill in Masonry, and continued very capable of rebuilding the
holy Temple and city of Salem upon its old founda-
tions, which was ordered by the edict or decree of
the grand CYRUS, according to GOD's Word, that
had foretold his exaltation and this decree : And

and the new town on the west side, much larger than the old,
and built in order to make this capital exceed old Niniveh, tho'
it never had so many inhabitants by one half. The river was
begirt with banks of brick, as thick as the city walls, in length
twenty miles, viz. fifteen miles within the city, and two miles
and a half above and below it, to keep the water within its channel; and each street that cross'd the river had a brazen gate
leading down to the water on both banks; and west of the city
was a prodigious lake, in compass 160 miles, with a canal from
the river into it, to prevent inundations in the summer.

In the old town, was the old tower of Babel, at the foundation
a square of half a mile in compass, consisting of eight square
towers built over each other, with stairs on the out-side round it,
going up to the observatory on the top, 600 foot high (which is
19 foot higher than the highest pyramid) whereby they became
the first Astronomers. And in the rooms of the grand tower,
with arched roofs, supported by pillars 75 foot high, the idola-
trous worship of their God BELUS was perform'd, till now, that
this mighty Mason and Monarch erected round this ancient pile
a temple of two furlongs on every side, or a mile in compass ;
where he lodg'd the sacred trophies of SOLOMON's TEMPLE, and the
golden image 90 foot high, that he had consecrated in the plains
of Dura, as were formerly in the tower lodg'd many other golden
images, and many precious things, that were afterwards all
seized by XERXES, and amounted to above 21 millions sterling.

CYRUS, having constituted ZERUBBABEL, the son of
SALATHIEL (of the seed of DAVID, by NATHAN, the
brother of SOLOMON, whose royal family was now
extinct,) the head, or Prince of the captivity, and
the leader of the Jews and Israelites returning to
Jerusalem, they began to lay the foundation of the
second Temple, and would have soon finished it, if
CYRUS had lived; but at length they put on the
cape-stone, in the 6th year of DARIUS, the Persian
monarch, when it was dedicated with joy and many
great sacrifices by ZERUBBABEL, the Prince and
General Master Mason of the Jews, about 20 years
after the decree of the Grand CYRUS. And though
this Temple of ZERUBBABEL came far short of SOLO-
MON's Temple, was not so richly adorned with gold
and diamonds, and all manner of precious stones,
nor had the Shechinah and the holy relicks of MOSES
in it, &c., yet being raised exactly upon SOLOMON's

And when all was finish'd, King NEBUCHADNEZZAR walking in
state in his hanging-gardens, and from thence taking a review
of the whole city, proudly boasted of this his mighty work;
saying, is not this great Babylon, that I have built for the house
of the Kingdom, by the might of my power, and for the honour
of my Majesty? but had his pride immediately rebuk'd by a
voice from Heaven, and punish'd by brutal madness for seven
years, until he gave glory to the God of Heaven, the Omnipotent
Architect of the Universe, which he publish'd by a decree thro'
all his empire, and dy'd next year, before his great Babylon was
little more than half inhabited (tho' he had led many nations
captive for that purpose); nor was it ever fully peopled; for in
25 years after his death, the Grand CYRUS conquer'd it, and
remov'd the throne to Shushan in Persia.

foundation, and according to his model, it was still the most regular, symmetrical, and glorious edifice in the whole world, as the enemies of the Jews have often testified and acknowledged.

At length the Royal Art was carried into Greece, whose inhabitants have left us no evidence of such improvements in Masonry, prior to SOLOMON'S Temple ;* for their most ancient buildings, as the Citadel of Athens, with the Parthenon, or Temple of Minerva, the Temples also of Theseus, of Jupiter Olympius, &c., their porticos also, and forums, their theatres and gymnasiums, their public halls, curious bridges, regular fortifications, stout ships of war, and stately palaces, were all erected after the Temple of SOLOMON, and most of them even after the Temple of ZERUBBABEL.

Nor do we find the Grecians arrived to any considerable knowledge in Geometry before the great THALES MILESIUS, the philosopher, who died in the reign of BELSHAZZAR, and the time of the Jewish captivity. But his scholar, the greater PYTHAGORAS, proved the author of the 47th Proposition of

---

* The Grecians having been long degenerated into barbarity, forgetting their original skill in Masonry, (which their forefathers brought from Assyria) by their frequent mixtures with other barbarous nations, their mutual invasions, and wasting, bloody wars ; until by travelling and corresponding with the Asiatics and Egyptians, they reviv'd their knowledge in Geometry and Masonry both, though few of the Grecians had the honour to own it.

Euclid's first book, which, if duly observed, is
the foundation of all Masonry, sacred, civil, and
military.*

The people of Lesser Asia about this time gave
large encouragement to Masons for erecting all
sorts of sumptuous buildings, one of which must not
be forgot, being usually reckoned the fourth of the
seven wonders of the world, viz : the Mausoleum, or
Tomb of MAUSOLUS, King of Caria, between Lycia
and Jonia, at Halicarnassus, on the side of Mount
Taurus, in that kingdom, at the command of ARTE-
MISIA, his mournful widow, as the splendid testimony of her love to him, built of the most curious
marble, in circuit 411 foot, in height 25 cubits, surrounded with 26 columns of the most famous sculpture, and the whole open on all sides, with arches
73 foot wide, performed by the four principal Master Masons and engravers of those times, viz : the
east side by SCOPAS, the west by LEOCHARES, the
north by BRIAX, and the south by TIMOTHEUS.

But after PYTHAGORAS, Geometry became the

* PYTHAGORAS travell'd into Egypt the year that THALES dy'd,
and living there among the Priests 22 years, became expert in
Geometry, and in all the Egyptian learning, until he was cap-
tured by CAMBYSES, King of Persia, and sent to Babylon, where
he was much conversant with the Chaldean Magi, and the learned
Babylonish Jews, from whom he borrow'd great knowledge, that
render'd him very famous in Greece and Italy, where afterwards
he flourish'd and dy'd ; when MORDECAI was the prime Minister
of State to AHASHUERUS King of Persia, and ten years after ZE-
RUBBABEL's Temple was finish'd.

darling study of Greece, where many learned philosophers arose, some of whom invented sundry Propositions, or Elements of Geometry, and reduced them to the use of the mechanical arts.* Nor need we doubt that Masonry kept pace with Geometry ; or rather, always followed it in proportioned gradual improvements, until the wonderful EUCLID of Tyre flourished at Alexandria, who, gathering up the scattered elements of Geometry, digested them into a method that was never yet mended, (and for which his name will be ever celebrated) under the patronage of PTOLOMEUS, the son of LAGUS, King of Egypt, one of the immediate successors of ALEXANDER the Great.

And as the noble science came to be more methodically taught, the Royal Art was the more generally esteemed and improved among the Grecians, who at length arrived to the same skill and magnificence in it with their teachers, the Asiatics and Egyptians.

The next King of Egypt, PTOLOMEUS PHILADELPHUS, that great improver of the liberal arts and of

* Or borrow'd from other nations their pretended inventions, as ANAXAGORAS, OENOPIDES, BRISO, ANTIPHO, DEMOCRITUS, HIPPOCRATES, and THEODORUS CYRENÆUS, the Master of the divine PLATO, who amplify'd Geometry, and published the Arts Analytic ; from whose Academy came forth a vast number, that soon dispers'd their knowledge to distant parts, as LEODAMUS, THRÆTETUS, ARCHYTAS, LEON, EUDOXUS, MENAICHMUS, and XENOCRATES, the Master of ARISTOTLE, from whose Academy also came forth EUDEMUS, THEOPHRASTUS, ARISTÆUS, ISIDORUS, HYPSICLES, and many others.

all useful knowledge, who gathered the greatest library upon earth, and had the Old Testament (at least the Pentateuch) first translated into Greek, became an excellent architect and General Master Mason, having, among his other great buildings, erected the famous Tower of Pharos,* the fifth of the seven wonders of the world.

We may readily believe that the African nations, even to the Atlantick shore, did soon imitate Egypt in such improvements, though history fails, and there are no travellers encouraged to discover the valuable remains in Masonry of those once renowned nations.

Nor should we forget the learned Island of Sicily, where the prodigious Geometrician ARCHIMEDES did flourish,† and was unhappily slain when Syra-

---

* On an Island near Alexandria, at one of the mouths of the Nile, of wonderful height and most cunning workmanship, and all of the finest marble, and it cost 800 talents, or about 480,000 crowns. The Master of Work, under the King, was SISTRATUS, a most ingenious Mason ; and it was afterwards much admired by JULIUS CÆSAR, who was a good judge of most things, though chiefly conversant in war and politicks. It was intended as a light-house for the harbor of Alexandria, from which the light-houses in the Mediterranean were often called Pharos. Though some, instead of this, mention as the fifth wonder the great Obelisk of SEMIRAMIS, 150 foot high, and 24 foot square at bottom, or 90 foot in circuit at the ground, all one intire stone, rising pyramidically, brought from Armenia to Babylon about the time of the siege of Troy, if we may believe the history of SEMIRAMIS.

† While ERATOSTHENES and CONON flourished in Greece, who were succeeded by the excellent APOLLONIUS of Perga, and many

antidote
before   Ancients &
Moderns   perspective

cuse was taken by MARCELLUS, the Roman General;
for from Sicily, as well as from Greece, Egypt and
Asia, the ancient Romans learned both the science
and the art, what they knew before being either
mean or irregular ; but as they subdued the nations,
they made mighty discoveries in both ; and, like wise
men, led captive, not the body of the people, but the
arts and sciences, with the most eminent professors
and practitioners, to Rome, which thus became the
center of learning, as well as of imperial power, until they advanced to their zenith of glory, under
AUGUSTUS CÆSAR, (in whose reign was born GOD'S
MESSIAH, the great Architect of the Church,) who,
having laid the world quiet, by proclaiming universal peace, highly encouraged those dexterous artists
that had been bred in the Roman liberty, and their
learned scholars and pupils ; but particularly the
great VITRUVIUS, the father of all true architects to
this day.

Therefore it is rationally believed that the glorious AUGUSTUS became the Grand Master of the
Lodge at Rome, having, besides his patronizing
VITRUVIUS, much promoted the welfare of the Fellow Craftsmen, as appears by the many magnificent
buildings of his reign, the remains of which are the
pattern and standard of true Masonry in all future

more before the birth of CHRIST, who, though not working
Masons, yet were good Surveyors ; or at least cultivated Geometry, which is the solid basis of true Masonry, and its rule.

times, as they are indeed an epitome of the Asiatic, Egyptian, Grecian, and Sicilian architecture, which we often express by the name of the Augustan style, and which we are now only endeavouring to imitate, and have not yet arrived to its perfection.

The old records of Masons afford large hints of their Lodges from the beginning of the world, in the polite nations, especially in times of peace, and when the civil powers, abhorring tyranny and slavery, gave due scope to the bright and free genius of their happy subjects; for then always Masons, above all other artists, were the favourites of the eminent, and became necessary for their grand undertakings in any sort of materials, not only in stone, brick, timber, plaister, but even in cloth or skins, or whatever was used for tents, and for the various sorts of architecture.

Nor should it be forgot that painters also and statuaries* were always reckoned good Masons, as

* For it was not without good reason the ancients thought that the rules of the beautiful proportions in building were copied or taken from the proportions of the body natural. Hence PHIDIAS is reckoned in the number of ancient Masons, for erecting the statue of the goddess NEMESIS at Rhamnus, 10 cubits high, and that of MINERVA at Athens, 26 cubits high; and that of JUPITER OLYMPIUS, sitting in his temple in Achaia, between the cities of Elis and Pisa, made of innumerable small pieces of porphyry, so exceeding grand and proportioned that it was reckoned one of the seven wonders, as the famous Colossus at Rhodes was another, and the greatest statue that ever was erected, made of metal, and dedicated to the sun, 70 cubits high, like a great tower at a distance, at the entry of an harbour, striding wide

2*

much as builders, stone-cutters, bricklayers, carpenters, joiners, upholders, or tent-makers, and a vast
many other craftsmen that could be named, who
perform according to Geometry and the rules of
building ; though none since HIRAM ABIF has been
renowned for cunning in all parts of Masonry ; and
of this enough.

But among the heathen, while the noble science
Geometry* was duly cultivated, both before and
after the reign of AUGUSTUS, even till the fifth cen-
tury of the Christian æra, Masonry was had in
great esteem and veneration ; and while the Roman
empire continued in its glory, the Royal Art was
carefully propagated, even to the Ultima Thule, and
a Lodge erected in almost every Roman garrison ;
whereby they generously communicated their cunning to the northern and western parts of Europe,
which had grown barbarous before the Roman con-

---

enough for the largest ships under sail, built in 12 years by
CARES, a famous Mason and statuary of Sicyon, and scholar to
the great LYSIPPUS of the same fraternity. This mighty Colossus,
after standing 56 years, fell by an earthquake, and lay in ruines,
the wonder of the world, till Anno Dom. 600, when the Soldan
of Egypt carried off its relicks, which loaded 900 camels.

* By MENELAUS, CLAUDIUS, PTOLOMEUS, (who was also the Prince
of Astronomers) PLUTARCH, EUTOCIUS (who recites the inventions
of PHILO, DIOCLES, NICOMEDES, SPHORUS, and HERON, the learned
mechanick,) KTESIBIUS also, the inventor of pumps (celebrated by
VITRUVIUS, PROCLUS, PLINY, and ATHENÆUS) and GEMINUS, also
equalled by some to EUCLID ; so DIOPHANTUS, NICOMACHUS, SE-
RENUS, PROCLUS, PAPPUS, THEON, &c., all Geometricians, and the
illustrious cultivators of the mechanical arts.

quest, though we know not certainly how long ; because some think there are a few remains of good Masonry before that period in some parts of Europe, raised by the original skill that the first colonies brought with them, as the Celtic edifices, erected by the ancient Gauls, and by the ancient Britains too, who were a colony of the Celtes, long before the Romans invaded this island.*

But when the Goths and Vandals, that had never been conquered by the Romans, like a general deluge over-ran the Roman empire, with warlike rage and gross ignorance they utterly destroyed many of the finest edifices, and defaced others, very few escaping, as the Asiatic and African nations fell under the same calamity by the conquests of the Mahometans, whose grand design is only to convert the world by fire and sword, instead of cultivating the arts and sciences.

Thus, upon the declension of the Roman empire,

---

* The natives within the Roman colonies might be first instructed in building of citadels and bridges, and other fortifications necessary ; and afterwards, when their settlement produced peace, and liberty, and plenty, the aborigines did soon imitate their learned and polite conquerors in Masonry, having then leisure and a disposition to raise magnificent structures. Nay, even the ingenious of the neighbouring nations not conquered, learnt much from the Roman garrisons in times of peace and open correspondence, when they became emulous of the Roman glory, and thankful that their being conquered was the means of recovering them from ancient ignorance and prejudices, when they began to delight in the Royal Art.

when the British garrisons were drained, the Angles and other lower Saxons, invited by the ancient Britons to come over and help them against the Scots and Picts, at length subdued the south part of this island, which they called England, or Land of the Angles, who, being akin to the Goths, or rather a sort of Vandals, of the same warlike disposition, and as ignorant heathens, encouraged nothing but war, till they became Christians; and then too late lamented the ignorance of their fathers in the great loss of Roman Masonry, but knew not how to repair it.

Yet, becoming a free people, (as the old Saxon laws testify) and having a disposition for Masonry, they soon began* to imitate the Asiatics, Grecians, and Romans, in erecting of Lodges and encouraging

* No doubt several Saxon and Scotish Kings, with many of the nobility, great gentry, and eminent clergy, became the Grand Masters of those early Lodges, from a mighty zeal then prevalent for building magnificent Christian temples; which would also prompt them to inquire after the laws, charges, regulations, customs, and usages of the ancient Lodges, many of which might be preserved by tradition, and all of them very likely in those parts of the British Islands that were not subdued by the Saxons, from whence in time they might be brought, and which the Saxons were more fond of, than careful to revive Geometry and Roman Masonry; as many in all ages have been more curious and careful about the laws, forms, and usages of their respective societies, than about the arts and sciences thereof.

But neither what was convey'd, nor the manner how, can be communicated by writing, as no man can indeed understand it without the key of a Fellow Craft.

of Masons, being taught not only from the faithful traditions and valuable remains of the Britons, but even by foreign Princes, in whose dominions the Royal Art had been preserved much from Gothic ruins, particularly by CHARLES MARTELL, King of France, who, according to the old records of Masons, sent over several expert craftsmen and learned architects into England, at the desire of the Saxon kings ; so that during the heptarchy, the Gothic architecture was as much encouraged here as in other Christian lands.

And though the many invasions of the Danes occasioned the loss of many records, yet in times of truce or peace they did not hinder much the good work, though not performed according to the Augustan style ; nay, the vast expence laid out upon it, with the curious inventions of the artists to supply the Roman skill, doing the best they could, demonstrate their esteem and love for the Royal Art, and have rendered the Gothic buildings venerable, though not imitable by those that relish the ancient architecture.

And after the Saxons and Danes were conquered by the Normans, as soon as the wars ended and peace was proclaimed, the Gothic Masonry was encouraged, even in the reign of the Conqueror,* and

---

o WILLIAM the Conqueror built the Tower of London, and many strong castles in the country, with several religious edifices, whose example was followed by the nobility and clergy,

of his son King WILLIAM RUFUS, who built Westminster Hall, the largest one room perhaps in the
earth.

Nor did the Barons' wars, nor the many bloody
wars of the subsequent Norman kings, and their
contending branches, much hinder the most sumptuous and lofty buildings of those times, raised by
the great clergy, (who, enjoying large revenues,
could well bear the expence,) and even by the Crown
too ; for we read King Edward III. had an officer
called the King's Free Mason, or General Surveyor
of his buildings, whose name was HENRY YEVELE,
employed by that king to build several abbeys, and
St. Stephen's Chappel at Westminster, where the
House of Commons now sit in Parliament.

But for the further instruction of candidates and
younger brethren, a certain record of Freemasons,
written in the reign of King EDWARD IV. of the
Norman line, gives the following account, viz ;

That though the ancient records of the brotherhood in England were many of them destroyed or
lost in the wars of the Saxons and Danes, yet King
ATHELSTAN, (the grandson of King ALFREDE the
Great, a mighty architect) the first anointed King
of England, and who translated the Holy Bible into
the Saxon tongue, when he had brought the land

particularly by ROGER DE MONTGOMERY, Earl of Arundel, the Archbishop of York, the Bishop of Durham, and GUNDULPH, Bishop
of Rochester, a mighty architect.

into rest and peace, built many great works, and encouraged many Masons from France, who were appointed overseers thereof, and brought with them the Charges and Regulations of the Lodges, preserved since the Roman times, who also prevailed with the king to improve the Constitution of the English Lodges according to the foreign model, and to increase the wages of working Masons.

That the said King's youngest son, Prince EDWIN, being taught Masonry, and taking upon him the Charges of a Master Mason, for the love he had to the said craft, and the honourable principles whereon it is grounded, purchased a free charter of King ATHELSTAN, his father, for the Masons having a correction among themselves, (as it was anciently expressed) or a freedom and power to regulate themselves, to amend what might happen amiss, and to hold a yearly communication and General Assembly.

That accordingly Prince EDWIN summoned all the Masons in the realm to meet him in a congregation at York, who came and composed a General Lodge, of which he was Grand Master ; and having brought with them all the writings and records extant, some in Greek, some in Latin, some in French, and other languages, from the contents thereof that Assembly did frame the Constitution and Charges of an English Lodge, made a law to preserve and observe the same in all time coming, and ordained good pay for working Masons, &c.

That in process of time, when Lodges were more frequent, the right worshipful the Master and Fellows, with consent of the lords of the realm, (for most great men were then Masons) ordained that for the future, at the making or admission of a brother, the Constitution should be read, and the Charges hereunto annexed, by the Master or Warden; and that such as were to be admitted Master Masons, or Masters of Work, should be examined whether they be able of cunning to serve their respective Lords, as well the lowest as the highest, to the honour and worship of the aforesaid art, and to the profit of their Lords; for they be their Lords that employ and pay them for their service and travel.

And besides many other things, the said record adds, that those Charges and laws of Freemasons have been seen and perused by our late Sovereign King HENRY VI. and by the Lords of his honourable Council, who have allowed them, and said that they be right good and reasonable to be holden, as they have been drawn out and collected from the records of ancient times.*

---

* In another manuscript more ancient, we read : "That when "the Master and Wardens meet in a Lodge, if need be, the "Sheriff of the county, or the Mayor of the city, or Alderman of "the town, in which the congregation is held, should be made

Now, though in the third year of the said King
HENRY VI., while an infant of about four years old,
the Parliament made an act that affected only the
working Masons, who had, contrary to the statutes
for labourers, confederated not to work but at
their own price and wages; and because such agreements were supposed to be made at the General
Lodges, called in the act Chapters and Congregations of Masons, it was then thought expedient to
level the said act against the said congregations;*

" Fellow and Sociate to the Master, in help of him against rebels,
" and for upbearing the rights of the realm.

" That Enter'd Prentices at their making were charg'd not to
" be thieves, or thieves maintainers; that they should travel
" honestly for their pay, and love their Fellows as themselves,
" and be true to the King of England, and to the realm, and to
" the Lodge.

" That at such congregations it shall be enquir'd whether any
" Master or Fellow has broke any of the articles agreed to. And
" if the offender, being duly cited to appear, prove rebel, and will
" not attend, then the Lodge shall determine against him that he
" shall forswear (or renounce) his Masonry, and shall no more
" use this craft; the which, if he presume for to do, the Sheriff
" of the county shall prison him, and take all his goods into the
" King's hands, till his grace be granted him and issued: For
" this cause principally have these congregations been ordain'd,
" that as well the lowest as the highest should be well and truly
" served in this art foresaid throughout all the kingdom of
" England.

" Amen, so mote it be."

* Tertio HENRICI SEXTI, cap. I. An. Dom. 1425.

Title—Masons shall not confederate themselves in chapters and
congregations.

" Whereas, by yearly congregations and confederacies, made
" by the Masons in their General Assemblies, the good course

yet when the said King HENRY VI. arrived to man's estate, the Masons laid before him and his Lords the above-mentioned Records and Charges, who, 'tis plain, reviewed them, and solemnly approved of them as good and reasonable to be holden : Nay, the said King and his Lords must have been incorporated with the Freemasons before they could make such review of the Records ; and in this reign, before King HENRY's troubles, Masons were much encouraged.   Nor is there any instance of executing that act in that or in any other reign since, and the Masons never neglected their Lodges for it, nor ever thought it worth while to employ their noble and eminent brethren to have it repealed ; because the working Masons that are free of the Lodge scorn to be guilty of such combinations; and the other free Masons have no concern in trespasses against the statutes for labourers.*

" and effect of the statutes for labourers be openly violated and " broken, in subversion of the law, and to the great damage of " all the Commons, our said Sovereign Lord the King, willing in " this case to provide a remedy, by the advice and assent afore- " said, and at the special request of the Commons, hath ordained " and established that such chapters and congregations shall not " be hereafter holden ; and if any such be made, they that cause " such chapters and congregations to be assembled and holden, " if they thereof be convict, shall be judged for felons, and that " the other Masons that come to such chapters and congregations " be punished by imprisonment of their bodies, and make fine " and ransome at the King's will."—Co. Inst. 8 p. 99.

    ° That act was made in ignorant times, when true learning was a crime, and Geometry condemn'd for conjuration; but it

The Kings of Scotland very much encouraged the Royal Art, from the earliest times down to the union of the crowns, as appears by the remains of glorious buildings in that ancient kingdom, and by the Lodges there kept up without interruption many hundred years, the records and traditions of which testify the great respect of those kings to this honourable fraternity, who gave always pregnant evidence of their love and loyalty, from whence sprung the old toast among Scots Masons, viz: God bless the King and the Craft!

Nor was the royal example neglected by the nobility, gentry, and clergy of Scotland, who joined in everything for the good of the craft and brotherhood, the kings being often the Grand Masters, until, among other things, the Masons of Scotland

cannot derogate from the honour of the ancient fraternity, who to be sure would never encourage any such confederacy of their working brethren. But by tradition it is believ'd that the Parliament men were then too much influenced by the illiterate clergy, who were not accepted Masons, nor understood architecture, (as the clergy of some former ages) and generally thought unworthy of this brotherhood ; yet thinking they had an indefeasible right to know all secrets, by vertue of auricular confession, and the Masons never confessing anything thereof, the said clergy were highly offended, and at first suspecting them of wickedness, represented them as dangerous to the State during that minority, and soon influenc'd the Parliament men to lay hold of such supposed agreements of the working Masons, for making an act that might seem to reflect dishonour upon even the whole worshipful fraternity, in whose favour several acts had been both before and after that period made

were impowered to have a certain and fixed Grand
Master and Grand Warden, who had a salary from
the Crown, and also an acknowledgment from every
new brother in the kingdom at entrance, whose
business was not only to regulate what might happen amiss in the brotherhood, but also to hear and
finally determine all controversies between Mason
and Lord, to punish the Mason, if he deserved it,
and to oblige both to equitable terms ; at which
hearings, if the Grand Master was absent, (who was
always nobly born) the Grand Warden presided.
This privilege remained till the civil wars, but is
now obsolete; nor can it well be revived until the
King becomes a Mason, because it was not actually
exerted at the union of the kingdoms.

Yet the great care that the Scots took of true
Masonry proved afterwards very useful to England,
for the learned and magnanimous Queen ELIZABETH,
who encouraged other arts, discouraged this ; because, being a woman, she could not be made a
Mason, though, as other great women, she might
have much employed Masons, like SEMIRAMIS and
ARTEMISIA.*

* ELIZABETH, being jealous of any assemblies of her subjects,
whose business she was not duly appriz'd of, attempted to break
up the annual communication of Masons, as dangerous to her
government; but as old Masons have transmitted it by tradition,
when the noble persons her Majesty had commissioned, and
brought a sufficient posse with them at York on St. JOHN's Day,
were once admitted into the Lodge, they made no use of arms,

But upon her demise, King JAMES VI. of Scotland, succeeding to the crown of England, being a Mason King, revived the English Lodges ; and as he was the first King of Great Britain, he was also the first Prince in the world that recovered the Roman architecture from the ruins of Gothic ignorance ; for, after many dark or illiterate ages, as soon as all parts of learning revived, and Geometry recovered its ground, the polite nations began to discover the confusion and impropriety of the Gothick buildings ; and in the fifteenth and sixteenth centuries, the Augustan stile was raised from its rubbish in Italy by BRAMANTE, BARBARO, SANSOVINO, SANGALLO, MICHAEL ANGELO, RAPHAEL URBIN, JULIO ROMANO, SERGLIO, LABACO, SCAMOZI, VIGNOLA, and many other bright architects ; but above all, by the great PALLADIO, who has not yet been duly imitated in Italy, though justly rivalled in England, by our great Master Mason, INIGO JONES.

But though all true Masons honour the memories of those Italian architects, it must be owned that the Augustan stile was not revived by any crowned head before King JAMES the Sixth of Scotland and First of England, patronized the said glorious INIGO

and return'd the Queen a most honourable account of the ancient fraternity, whereby her political fears and doubts were dispell'd, and she let them alone, as a people much respected by the noble and the wise of all the polite nations, but neglected the art all her reign.

JONES, whom he employed to build his Royal Palace of Whitehall ; and in his reign over all Great Britain, the Banqueting-house, as the first piece of it, was only raised, which is the finest one room upon earth ; and the ingenious Mr. NICHOLAS STONE performed as Master Mason under the architect JONES.

Upon his demise, his son King CHARLES I., being also a Mason, patronized Mr. JONES too, and firmly intended to have carried on his royal father's design of Whitehall, according to Mr. JONES's style ; but was unhappily diverted by the civil wars.* After the wars were over, and the royal family restored, true Masonry was likewise restored, espe-

* The plan and prospect of that glorious design being still preserv'd, it is esteem'd by skillful architects to excel that of any other palace in the known earth, for the symmetry, firmness, beauty and conveniency of architecture, as indeed all Master JONES's designs and erections are originals, and at first view discover him to be the architect : Nay, his mighty genius prevail'd with the nobility and gentry of all Britain, (for he was as much honour'd in Scotland as in England) to affect and revive the ancient stile of Masonry, too long neglected, as appears by the many curious fabricks of those times, one of which shall be now mention'd, the least, and perhaps one of the finest, the famous Gate of the Physic Garden at Oxford, rais'd by HENRY DANVERS, Earl of Danby, which cost his Lordship many hundred pounds, and is as curious a little piece of Masonry as ever was built there before or since, with the following inscription on the front of it, viz :

GLORIÆ DEI OPTIMI MAXIMI, HONORI CAROLI REGIS, IN USUM ACADEMLÆ ET REIPUBLICÆ, ANNO 1632.
HENRICUS COMES DANBY.

cially upon the unhappy occasion of the burning of London, Anno 1666; for then the city houses were rebuilt more after the Roman style, when King CHARLES II. founded the present St. Paul's Cathedral in London, (the old Gothick fabrick being burnt down) much after the style of St. Peter's at Rome, conducted by the ingenious architect, Sir CHRISTOPHER WREN. That king founded also his royal Palace at Greenwich, according to Mr. INIGO JONES's design, (which he drew before he died) conducted by his son-in-law, Mr. WEB; it is now turned into an hospital for seamen. He founded also Chelsea College, an hospital for soldiers; and at Edinburgh he both founded and finished his royal Palace of Halyrood House, by the design and conduct of Sir WILLIAM BRUCE, Bart., the Master of the Royal Works in Scotland;* so that, besides the tradition of old Masons now alive, which may be relied on, we have much reason to believe that King CHARLES II. was an accepted Freemason, as every one allows he was a great encourager of the craftsmen.

But in the reign of his brother King JAMES II., though some Roman buildings were carried on, the

* It was an ancient Royal Palace, and rebuilt after the Augustan style, so neat that by competent judges it has been esteem'd the finest house belonging to the Crown; and though it is not very large, it is both magnificent and convenient, both inside and outside, with good gardens, and a very large park, and all other adjacent accommodations.

Lodges of Freemasons in London much dwindled
into ignorance, by not being duly frequented and
cultivated.   But* after the revolution, Anno 1688,
King WILLIAM, though a warlike Prince, having a
good taste of architecture, carried on the aforesaid
two famous hospitals of Greenwich and Chelsea,
built the fine part of his royal Palace of Hampton
Court, and founded and finished his incomparable
Palace at Loo, in Holland, &c.   And the bright
example of that glorious Prince (who by most is
reckoned a Freemason) did influence the nobility,
the gentry, the wealthy and the learned of Great
Britain, to affect much the Augustan style, as appears by a vast number of most curious edifices

  ° But by the royal example of his brother, King CHARLES II.,
the city of London erected the famous Monument, where the
great fire began, all of solid stone, 202 foot high from the
ground, a pillar of the Dorick order, 15 foot diameter, with a
curious stair-case in the middle of black marble, and an iron
balcony on the top, (not unlike those of TRAJAN and ANTONINUS
at Rome) from whence the city and suburbs may be view'd,
and it is the highest column we know upon earth.   Its pedestal
is 21 foot square and forty foot high, the front of which is
adorn'd with most ingenious emblems in basso relievo, wrought
by that famous sculptor Mr. GABRIEL CIBBER, with large Latin
inscriptions on the sides of it, founded Anno 1671, and finish'd
Anno 1677.
  In his time also the Society of Merchant Adventurers rebuilt
the Royal Exchange of London, (the old one being destroy'd by
the fire) all of stone, after the Roman style, the finest structure
of that use in Europe, with the King's statue to the life, of white
marble, in the middle of the Square, (wrought by the famous
Master Carver and Statuary, Mr. GRINLIN GIBBONS, who was justly

erected since throughout the kingdom; for, when in the ninth year of the reign of our late Sovereign Queen ANNE, her Majesty and the Parliament concurred in an act for erecting 50 new parish churches in London, Westminster, and suburbs; and the Queen had granted a commission to several of the Ministers of State, the principal nobility, great gentry, and eminent citizens, the two Archbishops, with several other Bishops and dignified clergymen, to put the act in execution; they ordered the said

admir'd all over Europe, for his rivalling, if not surpassing the most fam'd Italian Masters,) on the pedestal of which is the following inscription, viz:

CAROLO II. CÆSARI BRITANNICO	TO CHARLES II. EMPEROR OF BRITAIN
PATRIÆ PATRI	FATHER OF HIS COUNTRY
REGUM OPTIMO CLEMENTISSIMO	BEST MOST MERCIFUL AND
AUGUSTISSIMO	AUGUST OF KINGS
GENERIS HUMANI DELICIIS	DELIGHT OF MANKIND
UTRIUSQUE FORTUNÆ VICTORI	IN ADVERSITY AND PROSPERITY UNMOV'D
PACIS EUROPÆ ARBITRO	UMPIRE OF EUROPE'S PEACE
MARIUM DOMINO AC VINDICI	COMMANDER AND SOVEREIGN OF THE SEAS
SOCIETAS MERCATORUM ADVENTUR. ANGLIÆ	THE SOCIETY OF MERCHANT ADVENTURERS OF ENGLAND.
QUÆ PER CCCC JAM PROPE ANNOS	WHICH FOR NEAR CCCC YEARS
REGIA BENIGNITATE FLORET	BY ROYAL FAVOUR FLOURISHETH
FIDEI INTEMERATÆ ET GRATITUDINIS ÆTERN.Æ	OF UNSHAKEN LOYALTY AND ETERNAL GRATITUDE
HOC TESTIMONIUM	THIS TESTIMONY
VENERABUNDA POSUIT	HAS IN VENERATION ERECTED
ANNO SALUTIS HUMANÆ MDCLXXXIV.	IN THE YEAR OF SALVATION MDCLXXXIV.

Nor should we forget the famous Theatre of Oxford, built by Archbishop SHELDON, at his sole cost, in that King's time, which, among his other fine works, was design'd and conducted also by Sir CHRISTOPHER WREN, the King's architect; for it is justly admir'd by the curious: and the Musæum adjoining to it, a fine building rais'd at the charge of that illustrious University, where there have been since erected several more Roman buildings, as

3

new churches to be raised according to the ancient
Roman style, as appears by those that are already
raised ; and the present honourable Commissioners
having the same good judgment of architecture, are
carrying on the same laudable grand design, and
are reviving the ancient style, by the order, countenance, and encouragement of his present Majesty
King GEORGE, who was also graciously pleased to
lay the first stone in the foundation of his parish
church of St. Martin's in Campis, on the south-east
corner, (by his Majesty's proxy for the time, the
present Bishop of Salisbury) which is now rebuilding, strong, large and beautiful, at the cost of the
parishioners.*

In short, it would require many large volumes to
contain the many splendid instances of the mighty

Trinity-College Chappel, Allhallows Church in High-street, Peck-
water-square in Christ-Church College, the new Printing-house,
and the whole of Queen's-College rebuilt, &c., by the liberal donations of some eminent benefactors, and by the publick spirit,
vigilancy, and fidelity of the heads of Colleges, who generally
have had a true taste of Roman architecture.

The learned University of Cambridge not having had the man-
agement of such liberal donations, have not so many fine struc-
tures; but they have two of the most curious and excellent in
Great-Britain of their kind, the one a Gothic building, King's-
College Chappel (unless you except King HENRY VII.'s Chappel in
Westminster-Abbey); and the other a Roman building, Trinity-
College Library.

   ° The Bishop of SALISBURY went in an orderly procession, duly
attended, and having levell'd the first stone, gave it two or three
knocks with a mallet, upon which the trumpets sounded, and a

influence of Masonry from the creation, in every age and in every nation, as could be collected from historians and travellers; but especially in those parts of the world where the Europeans correspond and trade, such remains of ancient, large, curious, and magnificent colonading, have been discovered by the inquisitive, that they can't enough lament the general devastations of the Goths and Mahometans; and must conclude that no art was ever so much encouraged as this, as indeed none other is so extensively useful to mankind.*

Nay, if it were expedient, it could be made appear, that from this ancient fraternity, the Societies

vast multitude made loud acclamations of joy; when his Lordship laid upon the stone a purse of 100 guineas, as a present from his Majesty for the use of the craftsmen. The following inscription was cut in the foundation stone, and a sheet of lead put upon it, viz:

D. S.	SACRED TO GOD
SERENISSIMUS REX GEORGIUS	HIS MOST EXCELLENT MAJESTY KING GEORGE
PER DEPUTATUM SUUM	BY HIS PROXY
REVERENDUM ADMODUM IN CHRISTO PATREM	THE RIGHT REVEREND FATHER IN CHRIST
RICHARDUM EPISCOPUM SARISBURIENSEM	RICHARD LORD BISHOP OF SALISBURY
SUMMUM SUUM ELEEMOSYNARIUM	HIS MAJESTY'S CHIEF ALMONER
ADSISTENTE (REGIS JUSSU)	ASSISTED (AT HIS MAJESTY'S COMMAND)
DOMINO THO. HEWET EQU. AUR.	BY SIR THOMAS HEWET KNIGHT
ÆDIFICIORUM REGIORUM CURATORE	OF HIS MAJESTY'S ROYAL BUILDINGS
PRINCIPALI	PRINCIPAL SURVEYOR
PRIMUM HUJUS ECCLESIÆ LAPIDEM	THE FIRST STONE OF THIS CHURCH
POSUIT	LAID
MARTIJ 19o ANNO DOM. 1721.	THIS 19TH OF MARCH ANNO DOMINI 1721
ANNOQUE REGNI SUI OCTAVO.	AND THE EIGHTH YEAR OF HIS REIGN.

* It were endless to recount and describe the many curious Roman buildings in Great-Britain alone, erected since the revival of Roman Masonry; of which a few may be here mentioned, besides those already spoken of, viz:

or Orders of the warlike knights, and of the religious too, in process of time did borrow many solemn usages ; for none of them were better instituted, more decently installed, or did more sacredly observe their laws and Charges, than the Accepted Masons have done, who, in all ages and in every

The Queen's House at Greenwich, ...	Belonging to the CROWN.
The great Gallery in Somerset-Gardens, . .	. The CROWN.
Gunnersbury-House near Brentford, Middlesex,	{ Possess'd by the Duke of QUEENSBURY.
Lindsay-House, in Lincoln's-Inn-Fields, . .	Duke of ANCASTER.
York-Stairs at the Thames in York-Buildings.	
St. Paul's-Church in Covent-Garden, with its glorious Portico.	
The Building and Piazza of Covent-Garden, . .	Duke of BEDFORD.
Wilton-Castle in Wiltshire, ...	. Earl of PEMBROKE.
Castle-Ashby in Northamptonshire, . . .	. Earl of STRAFFORD.
Stoke-Park in ditto, ...	. ARUNDEL Esq;
Wing-House in Bedfordshire, ...	. Hon. WM. STANHOPE, Esq;
Chevening-House in Kent, ...	. Earl STANHOPE.
Ambrose-Bury in Wiltshire, ...	. Lord CARLETON.

All designed by the incomparable INIGO JONES, and most of them conducted by him, or by his son-in-law Mr. WEB, according to Mr. JONES's designs.

Besides many more conducted by other architects, influenc'd by the same happy genius; such as,

Bow-Church Steeple in Cheapside, . . .	. Built by Sir CHRI. WREN.
Hotham-House in Beverley, Yorkshire, . .	. Sir CHARLES HOTHAM Bart.
Melvin-House in Fife, ...	. Earl of LEVIN.
Longleate-House in Wiltshire, ...	. Viscount WEYMOUTH.
Chesterlee-street-House in Durham County, .	. JOHN HEDWORTH Esq;
Montague-House in Bloomsbury, London, .	. Duke of MONTAGU.
Drumlanrig-Castle in Nithisdaleshire, . .	. Duke of QUEENSBURY.
Castle-Howard in Yorkshire, . . .	. Earl of CARLISLE.
Stainborough-House in ditto, . . .	. Earl of STRAFFORD.
Hopton-Castle in Linlithgowshire, . .	. Earl of HOPTON.
Blenheim-Castle at Woodstock, Oxfordshire, .	. Duke of MARLBOROUGH.
Chatsworth-Castle in Derbyshire, . . .	. Duke of DEVONSHIRE.
Palace of Hammilton in Clydsdaleshire, . .	. Duke of HAMMILTON.
Wanstead-House in Epping-Forest, Essex, .	. Lord CASTLEMAIN.
Duncomb-Park in Yorkshire, ...	. THOMAS DUNCOMB Esq;
Mereworth-Castle in Kent, ...	. Hon. JOHN FANE Esq;

nation, have maintained and propagated their con-
cernments in a way peculiar to themselves, which
the most cunning and the most learned cannot penetrate into, though it has been often attempted, while
they know and love one another, even without the
help of speech, or when of different languages.

Sterling-House near Sterling-Castle,	Duke of ARGYLE.
Kinross-House in Kinrossshire,	Sir WILLIAM BRUCE Bart.
Stourton-Castle in Wiltshire,	HENRY HOAR Esq;
Willbury-House in ditto,	WILLIAM BENSON Esq;
Bute-Castle in Isle of Bute,	Earl of BUTE.
Walpole-House near Lin Regis, Norfolk,	Hon. ROB. WALPOLE Esq;
Burlington-House in Pickadilly, St. James's, Westminster,	Earl of BURLINGTON.
Dormitory of King's-School, Westminster,	The CROWN.
Tottenham-Park in Wiltshire,	Lord BRUCE.

These three last are design'd and conducted by the Earl of
BURLINGTON, who bids fair to be the best architect of Britain, (if
he is not so already) and we hear his Lordship intends to publish the valuable remains of Mr. INIGO JONES, for the improvement
of other architects.

Besides more of the same Roman style, and yet many more in
imitation of it, which though they cannot be reduc'd to any certain style, are stately, beautiful, and convenient structures,
notwithstanding the mistakes of their several architects: and
besides the sumptuous and venerable Gothic buildings, past
reckoning, as cathedrals, parish-churches, chappels, bridges, old
palaces of the Kings, of the Nobility, of the Bishops, and the
gentry, known well to travellers, and to such as peruse the
histories of counties, and the ancient monuments of great families, &c., as many erections of the Roman style may be review'd
in Mr. CAMPBELL the architect's ingenious book, call'd Vitruvius
Britannicus: and if the disposition for true ancient Masonry
prevails, for some time, with noblemen, gentlemen, and learned
men, (as it is likely it will) this Island will become the Mistress
of the Earth, for designing, drawing, and conducting, and capable to instruct all other Nations in all things relating to the
Royal Art.

And now the free-born British nations, disentangled from foreign and civil wars, and enjoying the good fruits of peace and liberty, having of late much indulged their happy genius for Masonry of every sort, and revived the drooping Lodges of London, this fair metropolis flourisheth, as well as other parts, with several worthy particular Lodges, that have a quarterly communication and an annual Grand Assembly, wherein the forms and usages of the most ancient and worshipful fraternity are wisely propagated, and the Royal Art duly cultivated, and the cement of the brotherhood preserved; so that the whole body resembles a well built arch, several noblemen and gentlemen of the best rank, with clergymen and learned scholars of most professions and denominations, having frankly joined and submitted to take the Charges, and to wear the badges of a Free and Accepted Mason, under our present worthy Grand Master, the Most Noble Prince JOHN, Duke of Montague.

THE

Charges of a Free-Mason,

EXTRACTED FROM

THE ANCIENT **RECORDS** OF LODGES BEYOND SEA,

AND OF THOSE IN

ENGLAND, SCOTLAND AND IRELAND,

FOR THE USE OF THE LODGES IN LONDON.

*To be read at the making of New Brethren, or when the Master
shall order it.*

THE **General Heads**, VIZ:—I.

F GOD and RELIGION.

    II. Of the CIVIL MAGISTRATE, Supreme
    and Subordinate.

    III. Of LODGES.

    IV. Of MASTERS, WARDENS, FELLOWS, and
    APPRENTICES.

    V. Of the Management of the CRAFT in
    working.

VI. Of BEHAVIOUR, viz.

1. In the Lodge while CONSTITUTED.
2. After the Lodge is over and the BRETHREN not gone.
3. When Brethren meet without STRANGERS, but not in a LODGE.
4. In Presence of STRANGERS NOT MASONS.
5. At HOME and in the NEIGHBOURHOOD.
6. Towards a STRANGE BROTHER.

I.—Concerning God and Religion.

A Mason is oblig'd, by his Tenure, to obey the Moral Law ; and if he rightly understands the Art, he will never be a stupid ATHEIST, no[t] an irreligious LIBERTINE. But though in ancient Times Masons were charg'd in every Country to be of the Religion of that Country or Nation, whatever it was, 'tis now thought more expedient only to oblige them to that Religion in which all Men agree, leaving their particular Opinions to themselves ; that is, to be *good men and true*, or Men of Honour and Honesty, by whatever Denominations or Persuasions they may be distinguished ; whereby Masonry becomes the *Center* of *Union*, and the Means of conciliating true Friendship among persons that must have remain'd at a perpetual Distance.

II.—Of the Civil Magistrate, Supreme and Subordinate.

A Mason is a peaceable Subject to the Civil Powers wherever he resides or works, and is never to be concern'd in Plots and Conspiracies against the Peace and Welfare of the Nation, nor to behave himself undutifully to inferior Magistrates ; for as Masonry hath been always injured by War, Bloodshed, and Confusion, so ancient Kings and Princes have been much dispos'd to encourage the Craftsmen, because of their Peaceableness and Loyalty, whereby they practically answer'd the Cavils of their Adversaries, and promoted the Honor of the Fraternity, who ever flourish'd in Times of Peace. So that if a Brother should be a Rebel against the State, he is not to be countenanc'd in his Rebellion, however he may be pitied as an unhappy Man ; and, if convicted of no other Crime, though the loyal Brotherhood must and ought to disown his Rebellion, and give no Umbrage or Ground of political Jealousy to the Government for the time being they cannot expel him from the Lodge, and his Relation to it remains indefeasible.

III.—Of Lodges.

A Lodge is a Place where Masons assemble and work: Hence that Assembly, or duly organiz'd Society of Masons, is call'd a *Lodge*, and every Brother ought to belong to one, and to be subject to its By-laws and the General Regulations. It is either Particular or General, and will be best understood by attending it, and by the Regulations of the General or Grand Lodge hereunto annex'd. In ancient Times, no Master or Fellow could be absent from it, especially when warn'd to appear at it, without incurring a severe Censure, until it appear'd to the Master and Wardens, that pure Necessity hinder'd him.

The Persons admitted Members of a Lodge must be good and true Men, free-born, and of mature and discreet Age, no Bondmen, no Women, no immoral or scandalous Men, but of good Report.

IV.—Of Masters, Wardens, Fellows and Apprentices.

All Preferment among Masons is grounded upon real Worth and personal Merit only; that so the Lords may be well served, the Brethren not put to Shame, nor the Royal Craft despis'd: Therefore no Master or Warden is chosen by Seniority, but for his Merit. It is impossible to describe these things in writing, and every Brother must attend in his Place, and learn them in a way peculiar to This Fraternity: Only Candidates may know, that no Master should take an Apprentice, unless he has sufficient Imployment for him, and unless he be a perfect Youth, having no Maim or Defect in his Body, that may render him uncapable of learning the Art of serving his Master's LORD, and of being made a *Brother*, and then a *Fellow-Craft* in due time, even after he has served such a Term of Years as the Custom of the Country directs; and that he should be descended of honest Parents; that so, when otherwise qualify'd, he may arrive to the Honour of being the *Warden*, and then the *Master* of the Lodge, the

3*

Grand Warden, and at length the *Grand Master* of all the Lodges, according to his Merit.

No Brother can be a Warden until he has pass'd the part of a Fellow-Craft; nor a Master until he has acted as a Warden, nor Grand-Warden until he has been Master of a Lodge, nor GRAND MASTER unless he has been a Fellow-Craft before his Election, who is also to be nobly born, or a Gentleman of the best Fashion, or some eminent Scholar, or some curious Architect, or other Artist, descended of honest Parents, and who is of singular great Merit in the Opinion of the Lodges. And for the better, and easier, and more honourable Discharge of his Office, the Grand Master has a Power to chuse his own Deputy Grand Master, who must be then, or must have been formerly, the Master of a particular Lodge, and has the Privilege of acting whatever the Grand-Master, his Principal, should act, unless the said Principal be present, or interpose his Authority by a Letter.

* These Rulers and Governors, Supreme and Subordinate, of the ancient Lodge, are to be obey'd in their respective Stations by all the Brethren, according to the old Charges and Regulations, with all Humility, Reverence, Love, and Alacrity.

V.—Of the Management of the Craft in working.

All Masons shall work honestly on working Days, that they may live creditably on Holy Days; and the time appointed by the Law of the Land, or confirm'd by Custom, shall be observ'd.

The most expert of the Fellow-Craftsmen shall be chosen or appointed the Master, or Overseer of the Lord's Work; who is to be call'd *Master* by those that work under him. The Craftsmen are to avoid all ill Language, and to call each other by no disobliging Name, but Brother or Fellow; and to behave themselves courteously within and without the Lodge.

The Master knowing himself to be able of Cunning, shall

undertake the Lord's Work as reasonably as possible, and truly dispend his Goods as if they were his own; nor to give more Wages to any Brother or Apprentice than he really may deserve.

Both the Master and the Masons receiving their Wages justly, shall be faithful to the Lord, and honestly finish their Work, whether Task or Journey; nor put the Work to Task that hath been accustom'd to Journey.

None shall discover Envy at the Prosperity of a Brother, nor supplant him, or put him out of his Work, if he be capable to finish the same; for no man can finish another's Work so much to the Lord's profit, unless he be thoroughly acquainted with the Designs and Draughts of him that began it.

When a Fellow-Craftsman is chosen Warden of the Work under the Master, he shall be true both to Master and Fellows, shall carefully oversee the Work in the Master's Absence to the Lord's Profit; and his Brethren shall obey him.

All Masons employ'd shall meekly receive their Wages without Murmuring or mutiny, and not desert the Master till the Work is finish'd.

A Younger Brother shall be instructed in working, to prevent spoiling the Materials for want of Judgment, and for encreasing and continuing of Brotherly Love.

All the Tools used in working shall be approved by the Grand Lodge.

No Labourer shall be employ'd in the proper Work of Masonry; nor shall FREE MASONS work with those that are not free, without an urgent Necessity; nor shall they teach Labourers and unaccepted Masons, as they should teach a Brother or Fellow.

VI.—Of Behaviour, viz.
1.—In the Lodge while constituted.

You are not to hold private Committees, or separate Conversation, without Leave from the Master, nor to talk of any thing impertirent or unseemly, nor interrupt the Master or

Wardens, or any Brother speaking to the Master: Nor behave yourself ludicrously or jestingly while the Lodge is engaged in what is serious and solemn; nor use any unbecoming Language upon any Pretence whatsoever; but to pay due Reverence to your Master, Wardens, and Fellows, and put them to worship.

If any Complaint be brought, the Brother found guilty shall stand to the Award and Determination of the Lodge, who are the proper and competent Judges of all such Controversies, (unless you carry it by Appeal to the Grand Lodge) and to whom they ought to be referr'd, unless a Lord's Work be hinder'd the mean while, in which Case a particular Reference may be made; but you must never go to Law about what concerneth *Masonry*, without an absolute Necessity apparent to the Lodge.

2.—*Behaviour after the Lodge is over and the Brethren not gone.*

You may enjoy yourselves with innocent Mirth, treating one another according to Ability, but avoiding all Excess, or forcing any Brother to eat or drink beyond his Inclination, or hindering him from going when his Occasions call him, or doing or saying any thing offensive, or that may forbid an *easy* and *free* Conversation; for that would blast our Harmony, and defeat our laudable Purposes. Therefore no private Piques or Quarrels must be brought within the Door of the Lodge, far less any Quarrels about Religion, or Nations, or State Policy, we being only, as Masons, of the Catholick Religion above-mention'd; we are also of all Nations, Tongues, Kindreds, and Languages, and are resolv'd against *all Politicks*, as what never yet conduc'd to the Welfare of the Lodge, nor ever will. This *Charge* has been always strictly enjoin'd and observ'd; but especially ever since the Reformation in Britain, or the Dissent and Secession of these Nations from the Communion of Rome,

3.—*Behaviour when Brethren meet without Strangers, but not in a Lodge form'd.*

You are to salute one another in a courteous manner, as you will be instructed, calling each other *Brother*, freely giving mutual Instruction as shall be thought expedient, without being overseen or overheard, and without encroaching upon each other, or derogating from that Respect which is due to any Brother, were he not a Mason: For though all Masons are as Brethren upon the same Level, yet Masonry takes no Honour from a Man that he had before; nay, rather it adds to his Honour, especially if he has deserv'd well of the Brotherhood, who must give Honour to whom it is due, and avoid ill Manners.

4.—*Behaviour in Presence of Strangers not Masons.*

You shall be cautious in your Words and Carriage, that the most penetrating Stranger shall not be able to discover or find out what is not proper to be intimated ; and sometimes you shall divert a discourse, and manage it prudently for the Honour of the Worshipful Fraternity.

5.—*Behaviour at Home, and in your Neighbourhood.*

You are to act as becomes a moral and wise Man; particularly, not to let your Family, Friends, and Neighbours know the Concerns of the Lodge, &c., but wisely to consult your own Honour, and that of the Ancient Brotherhood, for Reasons not to be mention'd here. You must also consult your Health, by not continuing together too late, or too long from home, after Lodge Hours are past; and by avoiding of Gluttony or Drunkenness, that your Families be not neglected or injured, nor you disabled from working.

6.—*Behaviour towards a Strange Brother.*

You are cautiously to examine him, in such a Method as Prudence shall direct you, that you may not be impos'd upon

by an ignorant false Pretender, whom you are to reject with
Contempt and Derision, and beware of giving him any Hints
of Knowledge.

But if you discover him to be a true and genuine Brother,
you are to respect him accordingly ; and if he is in want, you
must relieve him if you can, or else direct him how he may
be reliev'd : You must employ him some Days, or else
recommend him to be employ'd. But you are not charged to
do beyond your Ability, only to prefer a poor Brother, that is
a Good Man and True, before any other poor People in the
same Circumstances.

Finally, All these CHARGES you are to observe, and also
those that shall be communicated to you in Another way ;
cultivating Brotherly-Love, the Foundation and Cape-stone,
the Cement and Glory of this ancient Fraternity, avoiding all
Wrangling and Quarrelling, all Slander and Backbiting, nor
permitting others to slander any honest Brother, but defend-
ing his Character, and doing him all good Offices, as far as is
consistent with your Honour and Safety, and no farther.   And
if any of them do you Injury, you must apply to your own or
his Lodge ; and from thence you may appeal to the Grand
Lodge at the Quarterly Communication, and from thence to
the Annual Grand Lodge, as has been the ancient laudable
Conduct of our Fore-fathers in every Nation ; never taking a
Legal Course, but when the Case cannot be otherwise decided,
and patiently listening to the honest and friendly Advice
of Master and Fellows, when they would prevent you going
to Law with Strangers, or would excite you to put a speedy
period to all Law-suits, that so you may mind the Affair of
Masonry with the more Alacrity and Success ; but with respect to Brothers or Fellows at Law, the Master and Brethren
should kindly offer their Mediation, which ought to be thankfully submitted to by the contending Brethren ; and if that
submission is impracticable, they must however carry on
their Process, or Law-Suit, without Wrath and Rancor, (not

in the common way,) saying or doing nothing which may hinder Brotherly Love, and good Offices to be renew'd and continu'd ; that all may see the Benign Influence of Masonry, as all true Masons have done from the Beginning of the World, and will do to the End of Time.

𝔄𝔪𝔢𝔫, 𝔰𝔬 𝔪𝔬𝔱𝔢 𝔦𝔱 𝔟𝔢.

POSTSCRIPT.

A Worthy Brother, learned in the Law, has communicated to the Author (while this Sheet was printing) the Opinion of the Great Judge Coke upon the Act against Masons, 3 Hen. VI. Cap. I., which is printed in this Book, Page 35, and which Quotation the Author has compar'd with the Original, viz.

C O K E's *Institutes*, THIRD PART, FOL. 99.

The Cause wherefore this Offense was made Felony, is for that the *good Course and Effect of the Statutes of Labourers were thereby violated and broken.* Now (sais my Lord Coke) all the Statutes concerning Labourers, before this Act, and where-unto this Act doth refer, are repeal'd by the Statute of 5 Eliz. Cap. 4. whereby the *Cause* and *End* of making this Act is taken away; and consequently this Act is become of no Force or Effect; for, *cessante ratione Legis, cessat ipsa Lex:* And the In-dictment of Felony upon this Statute must contain, that *those Chapters and Congregations were to the violating and breaking of the good Course and Effect of the Statutes of Labourers*, which now cannot be so alleg'd, because these Statutes be repealed. Therefore this would be put out of the *Charge of Justices of Peace*, written by Master Lambert, pag. 227.

This Quotation confirms the Tradition of old Masons, that this most learned Judge really belong'd to the ancient Lodge, and was a faithful Brother.

General Regulations,

Compiled first by Mr. GEORGE PAYNE, *Anno* 1720, when he was Grand-Master, and approv'd by the GRAND-LODGE on *St. John Baptist's* Day, *Anno* 1721, at *Stationer's-Hall*, LONDON; when the *most noble* PRINCE *John Duke of* MONTAGU was unanimously chosen our Grand-Master for the Year ensuing; who chose JOHN BEAL, M. D., his *Deputy* GRAND-MASTER; and { Mr. *Josiah Villeneau* } were chosen by the { Mr. *Thomas Morris, jun.* } Lodge GRAND-WARDENS. And now, by the Command of our said *Right Worshipful* GRAND-MASTER MONTAGU, the *Author* of this Book has compar'd them with, and reduc'd them to the ancient *Records* and immemorial *Usages* of the Fraternity, and digested them into this new Method, with several proper Explications, for the Use of the Lodges in and about *London* and *Westminster*.

I.

HE GRAND MASTER, or his *Deputy*, hath Authority and Right, not only to be present in any true Lodge, but also to preside wherever he is, with the Master of the Lodge on his Left-hand, and to order his Grand Wardens to attend him, who are not to act in particular Lodges as Wardens, but in his Presence, and at his Command; because there the Grand Master may command the Wardens of that Lodge, or any other Brethren he pleaseth, to attend and act as his Wardens *pro tempore*.

II. The Master of a particular Lodge has the Right and Authority of congregating the Members of his Lodge into a Chapter at pleasure, upon any Emergency or Occurrence, as well as to appoint the time and place of their usual forming; And in case of Sickness, Death, or necessary Absence of the Master, the Senior Warden shall act as Master *pro tempore*, if no Brother is present who has been Master of that Lodge before; for in that Case the Absent Master's Authority reverts to the last Master then present; though he cannot act until the said Senior Warden has once congregated the Lodge, or in his Absence the Junior Warden.

III. The Master of each particular Lodge, or one of the Wardens, or some other Brother by his Order, shall keep a Book containing their By-Laws, the Names of their Members, with a List of all the Lodges in Town, and the usual Times and Places of their forming, and all their Transactions that are proper to be written.

IV. No Lodge shall make more than Five New Brethren at one Time, nor any Man under the Age of Twenty-five, who must be also his own Master; unless by a Dispensation from the Grand-Master or his Deputy.

V. No Man can be made or admitted a Member of a particular Lodge, without previous notice one Month before given to the said Lodge, in order to make due Enquiry into the Reputation and Capacity of the Candidate; unless by the Dispensation aforesaid.

VI. But no Man can be enter'd a Brother in any particular Lodge, or admitted to be a Member thereof, without the unanimous Consent of all the Members of that Lodge then present when the Candidate is propos'd, and their Consent is formally ask'd by the Master; and they are to signify their Consent or Dissent in their own prudent way, either virtually or in form, but with Unanimity: Nor is this inherent Privi lege subject to a Dispensation; because the Members of a

particular Lodge are the best judges of it; and if a fractious
Member should be imposed on them, it might spoil their Harmony, or hinder their Freedom; or even break or disperse
the Lodge; which ought to be avoided by all good and true
Brethren.

VII. Every new Brother at his making is decently to cloath
the Lodge, that is, all the Brethren present, and to deposite
something for the Relief of indigent and decay'd Brethren, as
the Candidate shall think fit to bestow, over and above the
small Allowance stated by the By-Laws of that particular
Lodge; which Charity shall be lodged with the Master or
Wardens, or the Cashier, if the Members think fit to chuse one.

And the Candidate shall also solemnly promise to submit to
the Constitutions, the Charges, and Regulations, and to such
other good Usages as shall be intimated to them in Time and
Place convenient.

VIII. No Set or Number of Brethren shall withdraw or
separate themselves from the Lodge in which they were made
Brethren, or were afterwards admitted Members, unless the
Lodge becomes too numerous; nor even then, without a Dispensation from the Grand-Master or his Deputy: And when
they are thus separated, they must either immediately join
themselves to such other Lodge as they shall like best, with the
unanimous Consent of that other Lodge to which they go, (as
above regulated,) or else they must obtain the Grand Master's
Warrant to join in forming a new Lodge.

If any Set or Number of Masons shall take upon themselves
to form a Lodge without the Grand-Master's Warrant, the
regular Lodges are not to countenance them, nor own them
as fair Brethren and duly form'd, nor approve of their Acts
and Deeds; but must treat them as Rebels, until they humble
themselves, as the Grand-Master shall in his Prudence direct,
and until he approve of them by his Warrant, which must be
signify'd to the other Lodges, as the Custom is when a new
Lodge is to be register'd in the List of Lodges.

IX. But if any Brother so far misbehave himself as to render his Lodge uneasy, he shall be twice duly admonish'd by the Master or Wardens in a form'd Lodge; and if he will not refrain his Imprudence, and obediently submit to the Advice of the Brethren, and reform what gives them Offence, he shall be dealt with according to the By-Laws of that particular Lodge, or else in such a manner as the Quarterly Communication shall in their great Prudence think fit; for which a New Regulation may be afterwards made.

X. The Majority of every particular Lodge, when congregated, shall have the privilege of giving Instructions to their Master and Wardens, before the assembling of the Grand Chapter, or Lodge, at the three Quarterly Communications hereafter mention'd, and of the Annual Grand Lodge too; because their Masters and Wardens are their Representatives, and are suppos'd to speak their Mind.

XI. All particular Lodges are to observe the same Usages as much as possible; in order to which, and for cultivating a good Understanding among Free-Masons, some Members out of every Lodge shall be deputed to visit the other Lodges as often as shall be thought convenient.

XII. The GRAND LODGE consists of, and is form'd by the Masters and Wardens of all the regular particular Lodges upon Record, with the Grand Master at their Head, and his Deputy on his Left hand, and the Grand-Wardens in their proper Places, and must have a Quarterly Communication about Michaelmas, Christmas, and Lady-Day, in some convenient Place, as the Grand-Master shall appoint, where no Brother shall be present who is not at that time a Member thereof, without a Dispensation; and while he stays, he shall not be allow'd to vote, nor even give his Opinion, without Leave of the Grand Lodge ask'd and given, or unless it be duly ask'd by the said Lodge.

All Matters are to be determin'd in the Grand-Lodge by a

Majority of Votes, each Member having one Vote, and the Grand-Master having two Votes, unless the said Lodge leave any particular thing to the Determination of the Grand-Master for the sake of Expedition.

XIII. At the said Quarterly Communication, all Matters that concern the Fraternity in general, or particular Lodges, or single Brethren, are quietly, sedately, and maturely to be discours'd of and transacted: Apprentices must be admitted Masters and Fellow-Craft only here, unless by a Dispensation. Here also all Differences that cannot be made up and accommodated privately, nor by a particular Lodge, are to be seriously considered and decided: And if any Brother thinks himself aggriev'd by the Decision of this Board, he may appeal to the Annual Grand-Lodge next ensuing, and leave his Appeal in Writing, with the Grand-Master, or his Deputy, or the Grand-Wardens.

Here also the Master or the Wardens of each particular Lodge shall bring and produce a List of such Members as have been made, or even admitted in their particular Lodges since the last Communication of the Grand-Lodge: And there shall be a Book kept by the Grand-Master, or his Deputy, or rather by some Brother whom the Grand-Lodge shall appoint for Secretary, wherein shall be recorded all the Lodges, with their usual Times and Places of forming, and the Names of all the Members of each Lodge; and all the Affairs of the Grand-Lodge that are proper to be written.

They shall also consider of the most prudent and effectual methods of collecting and disposing of what Money shall be given to, or lodged with them in Charity, towards the Relief only of any true Brother fallen into Poverty or Decay, but of none else: But every particular Lodge shall dispose of their own Charity for poor Brethren, according to their own By-Laws, until it be agreed by all the Lodges (in a new Regulation) to carry in the Charity collected by them to the Grand Lodge, at the Quarterly or Annual Communication, in order to make a common Stock of it, for the more handsome Relief of poor Brethren.

They shall also appoint a Treasurer, a Brother of good worldly substance, who shall be a Member of the Grand-Lodge by virtue of his Office, and shall be always present, and have power to move to the Grand-Lodge any thing, especially what concerns his Office. To him shall be committed all Money rais'd for Charity, or for any other Use of the Grand-Lodge, which he shall write down in a Book, with the respective Ends and Uses for which the several Sums are intended; and shall expend and disburse the same by such a certain Order, sign'd, as the Grand-Lodge shall afterwards agree to in a new Regulation: But he shall not vote in chusing a Grand-Master or Wardens, though in every other Transaction. As in like manner the Secretary shall be a Member of the Grand-Lodge by virtue of his Office, and vote in every thing except in chusing a Grand-Master or Wardens.

The Treasurer and Secretary shall have each a Clerk, who must be a Brother and Fellow-Craft, but never must be a Member of the Grand Lodge, nor speak without being allow'd or desir'd.

The Grand-Master, or his Deputy, shall always command the Treasurer and Secretary, with their Clerks and Books, in order to see how Matters go on, and to know what is expedient to be done upon any emergent Occasion.

Another Brother (who must be a Fellow-Craft) should be appointed to look after the Door of the Grand-Lodge; but shall be no Member of it.

But these Offices may be farther explain'd by a new Regulation, when the Necessity and Expediency of them may more appear than at present to the Fraternity.

XIV. If at any Grand-Lodge, stated or occasional, quarterly or annual, the GRAND-MASTER and his Deputy should be both absent, then the present Master of a Lodge, that has

been the longest a Free-Mason, shall take the Chair, and preside as Grand-Master *pro tempore*, and shall be vested with
all his Power and Honour for the time; provided there is no
Brother present that has been Grand-Master formerly, or
Deputy Grand-Master; for the last Grand-Master present,
or else the last Deputy present, should always of right take
place in the absence of the present Grand-Master and his
Deputy.

XV. In the Grand-Lodge none can act as Wardens but the
Grand-Wardens themselves, if present; and if absent, the
Grand-Master, or the Person who presides in his Place, shall
order private Wardens to act as Grand-Wardens *pro tempore*,
whose Places are to be supply'd by two Fellow-Craft of the
same Lodge, call'd forth to act, or sent thither by the particular Master thereof; or if by him omitted, then they shall
be call'd by the Grand-Master, that so the Grand-Lodge may
be always compleat.

XVI. The Grand Wardens, or any others, are first to advise
with the Deputy about the Affairs of the Lodge or of the Brethren, and not to apply to the Grand-Master without the Knowledge of the Deputy, unless he refuse his concurrence in any
certain necessary Affair; in which Case, or in case of any Difference between the Deputy and the Grand Wardens, or
other Brethren, both parties are to go by Concert to the
Grand-Master, who can easily decide the Controversy and
make up the difference by virtue of his great Authority.

The Grand-Master should receive no Intimation of Business
concerning Masonry, but from his Deputy first, except in such
certain Cases as his Worship can well judge of; for if the
Application to the Grand-Master be irregular, he can easily
order the Grand-Wardens, or any other Brethren thus apply-
ing, to wait upon his Deputy, who is to prepare the Business
speedily, and to lay it orderly before his Worship.

XVII. No GRAND-MASTER, Deputy Grand-Master, Grand
Wardens, Treasurer, Secretary, or whoever acts for them, or

in their stead *pro tempore*, can at the same time be the Master or Warden of a particular Lodge; but as soon as any of them has honourably discharg'd his Grand Office, he returns to that Post or Station in his particular Lodge, from which he was call'd to officiate above.

XVIII. If the Deputy Grand-Master be sick, or necessarily absent, the Grand-Master may chuse any Fellow-Craft he please to be his Deputy *pro tempore:* But he that is chusen Deputy at the Grand-Lodge, and the Grand-Wardens too, cannot be discharg'd without the Cause fairly appear to the Majority of the Grand-Lodge; and the GRAND-MASTER, if he is uneasy, may call a Grand-Lodge on purpose to lay the Cause before them, and to have their Advice and Concurrence : In which case, the Majority of the Grand-Lodge, if they cannot reconcile the MASTER and his Deputy or his Wardens, are to concur in allowing the MASTER to discharge his said Deputy or his said Wardens, and to chuse another Deputy immediately; and the said Grand-Lodge shall chuse other Wardens in that Case, that Harmony and Peace may be preserved.

XIX. If the GRAND-MASTER should abuse his Power, and render himself unworthy of the Obedience and Subjection of the Lodges, he shall be treated in a way and manner to be agreed upon in a new Regulation; because hitherto the ancient Fraternity have had no occasion for it, their former Grand-Masters having all behaved themselves worthy of that honourable Office.

XX. The Grand-Master, with his Deputy and Wardens, shall (at least once) go round and visit all the Lodges about Town during his Mastership.

XXI. If the GRAND-MASTER die during his Mastership, or by Sickness, or by being beyond Sea, or any other way should be render'd uncapable of discharging his Office, the Deputy, or, in his Absence, the Senior Grand-Warden, or, in his Absence, the Junior, or, in his Absence, any three present Masters of Lodges, shall join to congregate the Grand-Lodge immediately, to advise together upon that Emergency, and to send two of their number to invite the *last* Grand-Master to resume his Office, which now in course reverts to him; or, if he refuse, then the *next last*, and so backward. But if no former Grand-Master can be found, then the *Deputy* shall act as *Principal* until another is chosen; or, if there be no Deputy, then the oldest Master.

XXII. The Brethren of all the Lodges in and about London and Westminster shall meet at an *Annual Communication* and *Feast*, in some convenient place, on *St. John Baptist's* Day, or else on *St. John Evangelist's* Day, as the Grand-Lodge shall think fit by a *new Regulation*, having of late Years met on St. John Baptist's Day: Provided,

The *Majority* of the Masters and Wardens, with the Grand-Master, his Deputy and Wardens, agree at their Quarterly Communications, three Months before, that there shall be a Feast, and a General Communication of all the Brethren: For if either the Grand-Master, or the Majority of the particular Masters, are against it, it must be dropt for that time.

But whether there shall be a Feast for all the Brethren, or not, yet the Grand-Lodge must meet in some convenient place *annually* on St. John's Day; or, if it be Sunday, then on the next Day, in order to chuse every Year a *new* Grand-Master, Deputy, and Wardens.

XXIII. If it be thought expedient, and the Grand-Master, with the Majority of the Masters and Wardens, agree to hold a Grand Feast, according to the ancient laudable Custom of Masons, then the Grand-Wardens shall have the care of preparing the Tickets, seal'd with the Grand-Master's Seal, of disposing of the Tickets, of receiving the Money for the Tickets, of buying the Materials of the Feast, of finding out a proper and convenient place to feast in, and of every other thing that concerns the Entertainment.

But, that the Work may not be too burthensome to the two Grand-Wardens, and that all Matters may be expeditiously and safely managed, the Grand-Master, or his Deputy, shall have power to nominate and appoint a certain number of Stewards, as his Worship shall think fit, to act in concert with the two Grand-Wardens; all things relating to the Feast being decided amongst them by a Majority of Voices, except the Grand-Master or his Deputy interpose by a particular Direction or Appointment.

XXIV. The Wardens and STEWARDS shall, in due time, wait upon the Grand-Master, or his Deputy, for Directions and Orders about the premisses; but if his Worship and his Deputy are sick, or necessarily absent, they shall call together the Masters and Wardens of Lodges to meet on purpose for their Advice and Orders; or else they may take the Matter wholly upon themselves, and do the best they can.

The Grand-Wardens and the Stewards are to account for all the Money they receive, or expend, to the Grand-Lodge, after Dinner, or when the Grand-Lodge shall think fit to receive their Accounts.

If the GRAND-MASTER pleases, he may in due time summon all the Masters and Wardens of Lodges, to consult with them about ordering the Grand Feast, and about any Emergency or accidental thing relating thereunto, that may require Advice; or else to take it upon himself altogether.

XXV. The Masters of Lodges shall each appoint one experienced and discreet Fellow-Craft of his Lodge, to compose a Committee, consisting of one from every Lodge, who shall meet to receive, in a convenient Apartment, every Person that brings a Ticket, and shall have Power to discourse him, if they think fit, in order to admit him, or debar him, as they shall see cause: *Provided* they send no Man away before they have acquainted all the Brethren within Doors with the Reasons thereof, to avoid Mistakes; that so no true Brother may

4

be debarr'd, nor a false Brother, or mere Pretender, admitted. This Committee must meet very early on St. John's Day at the place, even before any Persons come with Tickets.

XXVI. The Grand-Master shall appoint two or more TRUSTY BRETHREN to be Porters, or Door-keepers, who are also to be early at the Place, for some good Reasons; and who are to be at the Command of the Committee.

XXVII. The Grand-Wardens, or the Stewards, shall appoint beforehand such a Number of Brethren to serve at Table as they think fit and proper for that Work; and they may advise with the Masters and Wardens of Lodges about the most proper Persons, if they please, or may take in such by their Recommendation; for none are to serve that Day but Free and Accepted Masons, that the Communication may be free and harmonious.

XXVIII. All the Members of the Grand Lodge must be at the Place long before Dinner, with the Grand-Master, or his Deputy, at their Head, who shall retire, and form themselves. And this is done in order,

1. To receive any Appeals duly lodg'd, as above regulated, that the Appellant may be heard, and the Affair may be amicably decided before Dinner, if possible; but if it cannot, it must be delay'd till after the new Grand-Master is elected; and if it cannot be decided after Dinner, it may be delay'd, and referred to a particular Committee, that shall quietly adjust it, and make Report to the next Quarterly Communication, that Brotherly-Love may be preserv'd.

2. To prevent any Difference or Disgust which may be feared to arise that Day; that no Interruption may be given to the Harmony and Pleasure of the Grand Feast.

3. To consult about whatever concerns the Decency and Decorum of the Grand Assembly, and to prevent all Indecency and ill Manners, the Assembly being promiscuous.

4. To receive and consider of any good Motion, or any momentous and Important Affair, that shall be brought from the particular Lodges, by their Representatives, the several Masters and Wardens.

XXIX. After these things are discuss'd, the GRAND-MASTER and his Deputy, the Grand-Wardens, or the Stewards, the Secretary, the Treasurer, the Clerks, and every other Person shall withdraw, and leave the Masters and Wardens of the particular Lodges alone, in order to consult amicably about electing a new Grand-Master, or continuing the present, if they have not done it the Day before; and if they are unanimous for continuing the present Grand-Master, his Worship shall be call'd in, and humbly desir'd to do the Fraternity the Honour of ruling them for the year ensuing : And after Dinner it will be known whether he accepts of it or not: For it should not be discover'd but by the Election itself.

XXX. Then the Masters and Wardens, and all the Brethren, may converse promiscuously, or as they please to sort together, until the Dinner is coming in, when every Brother takes his Seat at Table.

XXXI. Some time after Dinner, the Grand-Lodge is form'd, not in the Retirement, but in the Presence of all the Brethren, who yet are not Members of it, and must not therefore speak until they are desir'd and allow'd.

XXXII. If the GRAND-MASTER of last Year has consented with the Master and Wardens in private, before Dinner, to continue for the year ensuing; then one of the Grand-Lodge, deputed for that purpose, shall represent to all the Brethren his Worship's good Government, &c. And, turning to him, shall, in the name of the Grand-Lodge, humbly request him to do the Fraternity the great Honour, (if nobly born, if not,) the great Kindness of continuing to be their Grand-Master for the Year ensuing. And his Worship declaring his Consent by a Bow or a Speech, as he pleases, the said deputed Member

of the Grand-Lodge shall proclaim him GRAND-MASTER, and all
the Members of the Lodge shall salute him in due Form.
And all the Brethren shall for a few Minutes have leave to
declare their Satisfaction, Pleasure, and Congratulation.

XXXIII. But if either the Master and Wardens have not
in private, this Day before Dinner, nor the Day before, desir'd
the *last* GRAND-MASTER to continue in the Mastership another
Year; or, if he, when desired, has not consented: Then,

The *last* Grand-Master shall nominate his successor for the
Year ensuing, who, if unanimously approved by the Grand-
Lodge, and if there present, shall be proclaim'd, saluted, and
congratulated the new GRAND-MASTER as above hinted, and
immediately install'd by the last Grand-Master, according to
Usage.

XXXIV. But if that Nomination is not unanimously approv'd, the new Grand-Master shall be chosen immediately
by Ballot, every Master and Warden writing his Man's Name,
and the last Grand-Master writing his Man's name too; and
the Man whose Name the last Grand-Master shall first take
out, casually or by chance, shall be Grand-Master for the
Year ensuing; and, if present, he shall be proclaim'd, saluted,
and congratulated, as above hinted, and forthwith install'd
by the last Grand-Master, according to Usage.

XXXV. The last Grand-Master thus continued, or the NEW
Grand-Master thus install'd, shall next nominate and appoint
his Deputy Grand-Master, either the last or a new one, who
shall be also declar'd, saluted and congratulated as above
hinted.

The GRAND-MASTER shall also nominate the new Grand-
Wardens, and, if unanimously approv'd by the Grand-Lodge,
shall be declared, saluted, and congratulated, as above hinted;
but if not, they shall be chosen by Ballot, in the same way as
the Grand-Master: As the Wardens of private Lodges are

also to be chosen by Ballot in each Lodge, if the Members thereof do not agree to their Master's Nomination.

XXXVI. But if the Brother, whom the present Grand-Master shall nominate for his Successor, or whom the Majority of the Grand-Lodge shall happen to chuse by Ballot, is, by Sickness or other necessary Occasion, absent from the Grand-Feast, he cannot be proclaim'd the new Grand-Master, unless the old Grand-Master, or some of the Masters and Wardens of the Grand-Lodge can vouch, upon the Honour of a Brother, that the said Person, so nominated or chosen, will readily accept of the said Office; in which case the old GRAND-MAS-TER shall act as Proxy, and shall nominate the Deputy and Wardens in his Name, and in his Name also receive the usual Honours, Homage, and Congratulation.

XXXVII. Then the GRAND-MASTER shall allow any Brother, Fellow-Craft, or Apprentice to speak, directing his Discourse to his Worship; or to make any Motion for the good of the Fraternity, which shall be either immediately consider'd and finish'd, or else referr'd to the Consideration of the Grand-Lodge at their next Communication, stated or occasional. When that is over,

XXXVIII. The Grand-Master or his Deputy, or some Brother appointed by him, shall harangue all the Brethren, and give them good Advice: And lastly, after some other Transactions, that cannot be written in any Language, the Brethren may go away or stay longer, as they please.

XXXIX. Every Annual Grand-Lodge has an inherent Power and Authority to make new Regulations, or to alter these, for the real benefit of this ancient Fraternity: Provided always that the old Land-Marks be carefully preserv'd, and that such Alterations and new Regulations be proposed and agreed to at the third Quarterly Communication preceding the Annual Grand Feast; and that they be offered also to the Perusal of all the Brethren before Dinner, in writing, even of the young-

est Apprentice; the Approbation and Consent of the Majority of all the Brethren present being absolutely necessary to
make the same binding and obligatory; which must, after
Dinner, and after the new Grand-Master is install'd, be solemnly desir'd; as it was desir'd and obtain'd for these Regulations, when propos'd by the Grand-Lodge, to about 150
Brethren, on St. John Baptist's Day, 1721.

POSTSCRIPT.

Here follows the Manner of constituting a New Lodge,
as practis'd by his GRACE the DUKE of WHARTON, the
present RIGHT WORSHIPFUL Grand=Master, according
to the ancient Usages of MASONS

New Lodge, for avoiding many Irregularities,
should be solemnly constituted by the Grand-Master, with his Deputy and Wardens; or, in the Grand-
Master's Absence, the Deputy shall act for his Worship, and shall chuse some Master of a Lodge to
assist him; or, in case the Deputy is absent, the
Grand-Master shall call forth some Master of a
Lodge to act as Deputy *pro tempore.*

The Candidates, or the new Master and Wardens, being
yet among the Fellow-Craft, the Grand-Master shall ask his
Deputy if he has examin'd them, and finds the Candidate Master well skill'd in the *noble Science* and the *royal Art*, and duly
instructed in our *Mysteries*, &c.

And the Deputy answering in the affirmative, he shall (by
the Grand-Master's order) take the Candidate from among his
Fellows, and present him to the Grand-Master; saying, *Right*

Worshipful Grand-Master: The Brethren here desire to be form'd into a new Lodge; and I present this my worthy Brother to be their Master, whom I know to be of good Morals and great Skill, true and trusty, and a Lover of the whole FRATERNITY, *wheresoever dispers'd over the face of the* EARTH.

Then the Grand-Master, placing the Candidate on his Left Hand, having ask'd and obtain'd the unanimous Consent of all the Brethren, shall say: *I constitute and form these good Brethren into a* NEW LODGE, *and appoint you the* MASTER *of it, not doubting of your Capacity and Care to preserve the* CEMENT *of the Lodge,* &c., with some other Expressions that are proper and usual on that Occasion, but not proper to be written.

Upon this, the Deputy shall rehearse the Charges of a Master, and the Grand-Master shall ask the Candidate, saying, *Do you submit to these Charges, as* MASTERS *have done in all Ages?* And the Candidate signifying his cordial Submission thereunto, the GRAND-MASTER shall, by certain significant Ceremonies and ancient Usages, install him, and present him with the Constitutions, the Lodge-Book, and the Instruments of his Office—not altogether, but one after another; and after each of them, the Grand-Master, or his Deputy, shall rehearse the short and pithy Charge that is suitable to the thing presented.

After this, the Members of this NEW LODGE, bowing all together to the Grand-Master, shall return his Worship Thanks, and immediately do their Homage to their NEW MASTER, and signify their Promise of Subjection and Obedience to him by the usual Congratulation.

The Deputy and the Grand-Wardens, and any other Brethren present, that are not Members of this NEW LODGE, shall next congratulate the NEW MASTER; and he shall return his becoming Acknowledgments to the Grand-Master first, and to the rest in their Order.

Then the Grand-Master desires the New Master to enter

immediately upon the Exercise of his Office, in chusing his Wardens: And the New Master, calling forth two Fellow-Craft, presents them to the Grand-Master for his Approbation, and to the New Lodge for their Consent. And that being granted,

The Senior or Junior Grand-Warden, or some Brother for him, shall rehearse the Charges of Wardens; and the Candidates being solemnly ask'd by the New Master, shall signify their submission thereunto.

Upon which the New Master, presenting them with the Instruments of their Office, shall, in due Form, install them in their proper Places; and the Brethren of that New Lodge shall signify their Obedience to the *new Wardens* by the usual Congratulation.

And this Lodge, being thus compleatly constituted, shall be register'd in the Grand-Master's Book, and by his Order notify'd to the other Lodges.

APPROBATION.

WHEREAS by the Confusions occasion'd in the SAXON, DANISH, and NORMAN Wars, the Records of Masons have been much vitiated, the Free Masons of England twice thought it necessary to correct their Constitutions, Charges, and Regulations; first in the Reign of King Athelstan the SAXON, and long after in the Reign of King Edward IV. the NORMAN: And Whereas the old Constitutions in England have been much interpolated, mangled, and miserably corrupted, not only with false Spelling, but even with many false Facts and gross Errors in History and Chronology, through Length of Time, and the Ignorance of Transcribers, in the dark, illiterate Ages, before the Revival of Geometry and ancient Architecture, to the great Offence of all the learned and judicious Brethren, whereby also the Ignorant have been deceiv'd.

And our late Worthy GRAND-MASTER, his Grace the Duke of Montagu, having order'd the Author to peruse, correct, and digest, into a new and better Method, the History, Charges, and Regulations of the ancient Fraternity; He has accordingly examin'd several Copies from Italy and Scotland, and sundry Parts of England, and from thence, (tho' in many things erroneous,) and from several other ancient Records of Masons, he has drawn forth the above-written new Constitutions, with the CHARGES and General REGULATIONS. And the Author having submitted the whole to the Perusal and Corrections of the late and present Deputy Grand-Masters, and of other learned Brethren; and also of the Masters and Wardens of particular Lodges at their Quarterly Communication: He did regularly deliver them to the late Grand-Master himself, the said Duke of Montagu, for his Examination, Correction, and Approbation; and his Grace, by the Advice of several Brethren, order'd the same to be handsomely printed for the use of the Lodges, though they were not quite ready for the Press during his Mastership.

Therefore We, the present Grand-Master of the Right Worshipful and most ancient Fraternity of Free and Accepted Masons, the Deputy Grand-Master, the Grand-Wardens, the Masters and Wardens of particular Lodges (with the Consent of the Brethren and Fellows in and about the Cities of London and Westminster) having also perused this Performance, Do Join our laudable Predecessors in our solemn Approbation

4*

thereof, as what We believe will fully answer the End proposed; all the valuable things of the old Records being retain'd, the Errors in History and Chronology corrected, the false Facts and the improper Words omitted, and the whole digested in a new and better Method.

And we ordain That these be receiv'd in every particular Lodge under our Cognizance, as the Only Constitutions of Free and Accepted Masons amongst us, to be read at the making of new Brethren, or when the Master shall think fit; and which the new Brethren should peruse before they are made.

PHILIP, DUKE OF WHARTON, **Grand-Master.**

J. T. DESAGULIERS, LL. D. and F. R. S., *Deputy Grand-Master.*

JOSHUA TIMSON,
WILLIAM HAWKINS, } *Grand-Wardens.*

And the *Masters* and *Wardens* of particular *Lodges*, viz.

I. THOMAS MORRIS, sen., *Master.*
JOHN BRISTOW,
ABRAHAM ABBOT, } *Wardens.*

II. RICHARD HAIL, *Master.*
PHILIP WOLVERSTON,
JOHN DOYER, } *Wardens.*

III. JOHN TURNER, *Master.*
ANTHONY SAYER,
EDWARD CALE, } *Wardens.*

IV. Mr. GEORGE PAYNE, *Master.*
STEPHEN HALL, M. D.,
FRANCIS SORELL, Esq., } *Wardens.*

V. Mr. MATH. BIRKHEAD, *Master.*
FRANCIS BAILY,
NICHOLAS ABRAHAM, } *Wardens.*

VI. WILLIAM READ, *Master.*
JOHN GLOVER,
ROBERT CORDELL, } *Wardens.*

VII. HENRY BRANSON, *Master.*
HENRY LUG,
JOHN TOWNSHEND, } *Wardens.*

VIII. *Master.*
JONATHAN SIBSON,
JOHN SHIPTON, } *Wardens.*

IX. GEORGE OWEN, M. D., *Master.*
EMAN BOWEN,
JOHN HEATH, } *Wardens.*

X. *Master.*
JOHN LUBTON,
RICHARD SMITH, } *Wardens.*

XI. FRANCIS, Earl of DALKEITH, *Master.*
Capt. ANDREW ROBINSON,
Col. THOMAS INWOOD } *Wardens*

XII. JOHN BEAL, M.D. and F.R.S., *Master.*
EDWARD PAWLET, Esq.,
CHARLES MORE, Esq., } *Wardens.*

XIII THOMAS MORRIS, jun., *Master.*
JOSEPH RIDLER,
JOHN CLARK, } *Wardens.*

XIV. THOMAS RORER, Esq., *Master.*
THOMAS GRAVE,
BRAY LANE, } *Wardens.*

XV. Mr. JOHN SHEPHERD, *Master.*
JOHN SENEX,
JOHN BUCLER, } *Wardens.*

XVI. JOHN GEORGES, Esq., *Master.*
ROBERT GRAY, Esq.,
CHARLES GRYMES, Esq., } *Wardens.*

XVII. JAMES ANDERSON, A.M.,
The **Author** of *this* **Book.** } *Master.*
GWINN VAUGHAN, Esq.,
WALTER GREENWOOD, Esq., } *Wardens*

XVIII. THOMAS HARBIN, *Master.*
WILLIAM ATTLEY,
JOHN SAXON, } *Wardens.*

XIX. ROBERT CAPELL, *Master.*
ISAAC MANSFIELD,
WILLIAM BLY, } *Wardens.*

XX. JOHN GORMAN, *Master.*
CHARLES GAREY,
EDWARD MORPHEY, } *Wardens*

THE MASTER'S SONG;

THE HISTORY OF MASONRY.

BY THE AUTHOR.

*To be sung with a Chorus, when the Master shall give leave, either one
Part only, or altogether, as he pleases.*

PART I.

I.

ADAM, the first of humane Kind,
  Created with Geometry
Imprinted on his Royal Mind,
  Instructed soon his Progeny
Cain and Seth, who then improv'd
  The lib'ral Science in the Art
Of Architecture, which they lov'd,
  And to their Offspring did impart.

II.

Cain a City fair and strong
  First built, and call'd it Consecrate,
From Enoch's Name, his eldest Son,
  Which all his Race did imitate.
But godly Enoch, of Seth's Loins,
  Two Columns rais'd with mighty Skill:
And all his Family enjoins
  True Colonading to fullfil.

III.

Our Father Noah next appear'd,
  A Mason too divinely taught;
And by divine Command uprear'd
  The Ark that held a goodly Fraught:

'Twas built by true Geometry,
  A Piece of Architecture fine;
Helpt by his Sons, in Number Three,
  Concurring in the Grand Design.

IV.

So from the gen'ral Deluge none
  Were sav'd, but Masons and their Wives;
And all Mankind from them alone
  Descending, Architecture thrives;
For they, when multiply'd amain,
  Fit to disperse and fill the Earth,
In Shinar's large and lovely Plain
  To Masonry gave second Birth.

V.

For most of Mankind were employ'd,
  To build the City and the Tow'r;
The Gen'ral Lodge was overjoy'd,
  In such Effects of Masons Pow'r;
'Till vain Ambition did provoke
  Their Maker to confound their Plot;
Yet tho' with Tongues confus'd they spoke,
  The learned Art they ne'er forgot.

CHORUS.

Who can unfold the Royal Art?
  Or sing its Secrets in a Song?
They're safely kept in Mason's Heart,
  And to the ancient Lodge belong.

[*Stop here to drink the present Grand-Master's
Health.*]

PART II.

I.

Thus when from Babel they disperse
  In Colonies to distant Climes,
All Masons true, who could rehearse
  Their Works to those of after Times;
King Nimrod fortify'd his Realm,
  By Castles, Towr's, and Cities fair:
Mitzra'm, who rul'd at Egypt's Helm,
  Built Pyramids stupendous there.

II.

Nor Japhet, and his gallant Breed,
  Did less in Masonry prevail;
Nor Shem, and those that did succeed
  To promis'd Blessings by Entail;
For Father Abram brought from Ur
  Geometry, the Science good;
Which he reveal'd, without demur,
  To all descending from his Blood.

III.

Nay, Jacob's Race at length were taught,
  To lay aside the Shepherd's Crook,
To use Geometry were brought,
  Whilst under Phar'oh's cruel Yoke;
'Till Moses Master-Mason rose,
  And led the Holy Lodge from thence,
All Masons train'd, to whom he chose,
  His curious Learning to dispense.

IV.

Aholiab and Bezaleel,
  Inspired Men, the Tent uprear'd:
Where the Shechinah chose to dwell,
  And Geometrick Skill appear'd:

And when these valiant Masons fill'd
  Canaan, the learn'd Phenicians knew
The tribes of Isra'l better skill'd
  In Architecture firm and true.

v.

For Dagon's House in Gaza Town
  Artfully propt by Columns two;
By Samson's mighty Arms pull'd down
  On Lords Philistian, whom it slew;
Tho' 'twas the finest Fabrick rais'd
  By Canaan's Sons, could not compare
With the Creator's Temple prais'd,
  For glorious Strength and Structure fair.

VI. .

But here we stop a while to toast
  Our Master's Health and Wardens both;
And warn you all to shun the Coast
  Of Samson's Shipwrackt Fame and Troth;
His Secrets once to Wife disclos'd,
  His Strength was fled, his Courage tam'd,
To Cruel Foes he was expos'd,
  And never was a Mason nam'd.

CHORUS.

Who can unfold the Royal Art?
  Or sing its Secrets in a Song?
They're safely kept in Mason's Heart,
  And to the Ancient Lodge belong.

  [*Stop here to drink the Health of the Master and
    Wardens of this particular Lodge*]

PART III.

I.

WE sing of Masons' ancient Fame,
   When fourscore Thousand CRAFTSMEN stood,
Under the Masters of great Name,
   Three Thousand and six Hundred good,
Employ'd by Solomon the Sire,
   And Gen'ral Master-Mason too;
As Hiram was in stately Tyre,
   Like Salem, built by Masons true.

II.

The Royal Art was then divine,
   The Craftsmen counsell'd from above,
The *Temple* did all Works outshine,
   The wond'ring World did all approve;
Ingenious Men, from every Place,
   Came to survey the glorious Pile;
And, when return'd, began to trace
   And imitate its lofty Style.

III.

At length the Grecians came to know
   Geometry, and learnt the Art,
Which great Pythagoras did show,
   And glorious Euclid did impart;
Th' amazing Archimedes, too,
   And many other Scholars good;
Till ancient Romans did review
   The Art, and Science understood.

IV.

But when proud Asia they had quell'd,
   And Greece and Egypt overcome,
In *Architecture* they excell'd,
   And brought the Learning all to Rome;

Where wise Vitruvius, Master prime
  Of Architects, the *Art* improv'd,
In great Augustus' peaceful Time,
  When *Arts* and *Artists* were belov'd

v.

They brought the Knowledge from the East;
  And as they made the Nations yield,
They spread it thro' the North and West,
  And taught the World the *Art to build;*
Witness their Citadels and Tow'rs,
  To fortify their Legions fine,
Their Temples, Palaces, and Bow'rs,
  That spoke the Masons' Grand Design.

vi.

Thus mighty Eastern Kings, and some
  Of Abram's Race, and Monarchs good,
Of Egypt, Syria, Greece, and Rome,
  True *Architecture* understood:
No wonder, then, if Masons join,
  To celebrate those Mason-Kings,
With solemn Note and flowing Wine,
  Whilst ev'ry Brother jointly sings.

CHORUS.

Who can unfold the Royal Art?
  Or sing its *Secrets* in a Song?
They're safely kept in Mason's Heart,
  And to the ancient Lodge belong.

[*Stop here to drink to the glorious Memory of Emperors, Kings, Princes, Nobles, Gentry, Clergy, and learned Scholars that ever propagated the Art.*]

PART IV.

I.

Oh! glorious Days for Masons wise,
  O'er all the Roman Empire when
Their Fame, resounding to the Skies,
  Proclaim'd them good and useful Men;
For many Ages thus employ'd,
  Until the Goths, with warlike Rage,
And brutal Ignorance, destroy'd
  The Toil of many a learned Age.

II.

But when the conqu'ring Goths were brought
  T' embrace the Christian Faith, they found
The Folly that their Fathers wrought,
  In loss of *Architecture* sound.
At length their Zeal for *stately Fanes*
  And wealthy Grandeur, when at Peace,
Made them exert their utmost Pains,
  Their Gothic Buildings to upraise.

III.

Thus many a sumptuous lofty Pile
  Was rais'd in every Christian Land,
Tho' not conform'd to Roman Style,
  Yet which did Reverence command;
The King and Craft agreeing still,
  In well-form'd Lodges to supply
The mournful Want of Roman Skill
  With their new sort of Masonry.

IV.

For many Ages this prevails,
  Their Work is *Architecture* deem'd;
In England, Scotland, Ireland, Wales,
  The Craftsmen highly are esteem'd,

By Kings, as MASTERS of the Lodge,
 By many a wealthy, noble PEER,
By Lord and Laird, by PRIEST and Judge,
 By all the People every where.

v.

So Masons' *ancient Records* tell,
 King ATHELSTAN, of Saxon Blood,
Gave them a Charter free to dwell
 In Lofty Lodge, with Orders good,
Drawn from old Writings by his Son,
 Prince Edwin, General Master bright,
Who met at York the Brethren soon,
 And to that Lodge did all recite.

VI.

Thence were their *Laws* and *Charges* fine
 In ev'ry Reign observ'd with Care,
Of SAXON, DANISH, NORMAN Line,
 Till British Crowns united were:
The Monarch First of this whole Isle
 Was learned James, a Mason King,
Who First of Kings reviv'd the Style
 Of Great Augustus: Therefore sing.

CHORUS.

Who can unfold the *Royal Art?*
Or sing its Secrets in a Song?
They're safely kept in Mason's Heart,
 And to the *ancient Lodge* belong.

 [*Stop here to drink to the happy Memory of all the
  Revivers of the ancient Augustan Style.*]

PART V.

I.

THUS tho' in Italy the Art
　From GOTHICK RUBBISH first was rais'd;
And great Palladio did impart
　A Style by Masons justly prais'd:
Yet here his mighty Rival Jones,
　Of British Architects the Prime,
Did build such glorious Heaps of Stones,
　As ne'er were matched since Cæsar's Time.

II.

King Charles the First, a Mason too,
　With several Peers and wealthy Men,
Employ'd him and his Craftsmen true,
　'Till wretched Civil Wars began.
But after Peace and Crown restor'd,
　Tho' London was in Ashes laid,
By Masons Art and good Accord,
　A finer London rear'd its Head.

III

King Charles the Second raised then
　The finest Column upon Earth,
Founded St. Paul's, that stately Fane,
　And Royal Change, with Joy and Mirth:
But afterwards the Lodges fail'd,
　'Till Great Nassau the Tast reviv'd,
Whose bright Example so prevail'd,
　That ever since the Art has thriv'd.

IV.

Let other Nations boast at will,
　Great Britain now will yield to none,
For true Geometry and Skill,
　In building Timber, Brick, and Stone;

For Architecture of each sort,
   For curious Lodges, where we find
The Noble and the Wise resort,
   And drink with Craftsmen true and kind.

v.

Then let good Brethren all rejoice,
   And fill their Glass with cheerful Heart;
Let them express with grateful Voice
   The praises of the wond'rous Art;
Let ev'ry Brother's Health go round,
   Not Fool or Knave, but Mason true;
And let our Master's Fame resound,
   The noble Duke of Montagu.

CHORUS.

Who can unfold the Royal Art?
   Or sing its Secrets in a Song?
They're safely kept in Mason's Heart,
   And to the ancient Lodge belong.

THE WARDEN'S SONG;

OR,

ANOTHER HISTORY OF MASONRY.

COMPOS'D SINCE THE MOST NOBLE PRINCE PHILIP, DUKE OF
WHARTON, WAS CHOSEN GRAND-MASTER.

BY THE AUTHOR.

To be sung and play'd at the Quarterly Communication.

I.

When e'er we are alone,
And ev'ry Stranger gone,
In Summer, Autumn, Winter, Spring,
Begin to play, begin to sing,
The mighty Genius of the lofty Lodge,
In ev'ry Age
That did engage
And well inspir'd the Prince, the Priest, the Judge,
The Noble and the Wise to join
In Rearing Masons' Grand Design.

II.

The Grand Design to rear,
Was ever Masons' Care,
From Adam down before the Flood,
Whose Art old Noah understood,
And did impart to Japhet, Shem, and Ham,
Who taught their Race
To build apace
Proud Babel's Town and Tow'r, until it came
To be admir'd too much, and then
Dispersed were the Sons of Men.

III.

But tho' their Tongues confus'd
In distant Climes they us'd,
They brought from Shinar Orders good,
To rear the Art they understood:
Therefore sing first the Princes of the Isles;
Next Belus Great,
Who fixt his Seat
In old Assyria, building stately Piles;
And Mitzraim's Pyramids among
The other subjects of our Song.

IV.

And Shem, who did instil
The useful wond'rous Skill
Into the Minds of Nations great:
And Abram next, who did relate
Th' Assyrian Learning to his Sons, that when
In Egypt's Land,
By Pharaoh's Hand,
Were roughly taught to be most skilful Men;
Till their Grand-Master Moses rose,
And them deliver'd from their Foes.

V.

But who can sing his Praise,
Who did the Tent upraise?
Then sing his Workmen true as Steel,
Aholiab and Bezaleel;
Sing Tyre and Sydon, and Phenicians old.
But Samson's Blot
Is ne'er forgot:
He blabb'd his Secrets to his Wife, that sold
Her Husband, who at last pull'd down
The House on all in Gaza Town.

VI.

But Solomon the King
With solemn Note we sing,
Who rear'd at length the Grand Design,
By Wealth, and Pow'r, and Art divine;
Helpt by the learned Hiram, Tyrian Prince,
By Craftsmen good,
That understood
Wise Hiram Abif's charming Influence:
He aided Jewish Masters bright,
Whose curious Works none can recite.

VII.

These glorious Mason Kings
Each thankful Brother sings,
Who to its Zenith rais'd the Art,
And to all Nations did impart
The useful Skill: For from the Temple fine,
To ev'ry Land,
And foreign Strand,
The Craftsmen march'd, and taught the Grand Design;
Of which the Kings, with mighty Peers,
And learned Men, were Overseers.

VIII.

Diana's Temple next,
In Lesser Asia fixt:
And Babylon's proud Walls, the Seat
Of Nebuchadnezar the Great;
The Tomb of Mausolus, the Carian King;
With many a Pile
Of lofty Style
In Africa and Greater Asia, sing,
In Greece, in Sicily, and Rome,
That had those Nations overcome.

IX.

Then sing Augustus too,
  The Gen'ral Master true,
Who by Vitrivius did refine,
And spread the Masons' Grand Design
Thro' North and West, till ancient Britons chose
    The Royal Art
    In ev'ry Part,
And Roman Architecture could disclose;
  Until the SAXONS warlike Rage
  Destroy'd the Skill of many an Age.

X.

At length the GOTHICK STYLE
  Prevail'd in Britain's Isle,
When Masons' Grand Design reviv'd,
And in their well form'd Lodges thriv'd,
Tho' not as formerly in Roman Days:
    Yet sing the Fanes
    Of SAXON DANES,
Of SCOTS, WELSH, IRISH; but sing first the Praise
  Of Athelstan and Edwin Prince,
  Our Master of great Influence.

XI.

And eke the NORMAN KINGS
  The British Mason sings;
'Till Roman Style revived there,
And British Crowns united were
In learned James, a Mason King, who rais'd
    Fine Heaps of Stones
    By Inigo Jones,
That rival'd wise Palladio, justly prais'd
  In Italy, and Britain too,
  For Architecture firm and true.

XII.

And thence in ev'ry Reign
Did Masonry obtain
With Kings, the Noble and the Wise,
Whose Fame, resounding to the Skies,
Excites the present Age in Lodge to join,
And Aprons wear
With Skill and Care,
To raise the Masons ancient Grand Design,
And to revive th' Augustan Style
In many an artful glorious Pile.

XIII.

From henceforth ever sing
The Craftsman and the King,
With Poetry and Musick sweet
Resound their Harmony compleat;
And with Geometry in skilful Hand,
Due Homage pay,
Without Delay,
To Wharton's noble Duke, our Master Grand:
He rules the Free-born Sons of Art,
By Love and Friendship, Hand and Heart.

CHORUS.

Who can rehearse the Praise,
In soft Poetick Lays,
Or Solid Prose, of Masons true,
Whose Art transcends the common View?
Their Secrets, ne'er to Strangers yet expos'd,
Preserv'd shall be
By Masons Free,
And only to the ancient Lodge disclos'd;
Because they're kept in Masons' Heart
By Brethren of the Royal Art.

5

THE FELLOW-CRAFT'S SONG.

BY OUR BROTHER CHARLES DELAFAYE, ESQ.

To be sung and play'd at the Grand-Feast.

I.

Hail, Masonry! thou Craft divine!
  Glory of Earth, from Heav'n reveal'd;
Which dost with Jewels precious shine,
  From all but Masons' Eyes conceal'd.

CHORUS.

Thy Praises due who can rehearse
In nervous Prose, or flowing Verse?

II.

As Men from Brutes distinguisht are,
  A Mason other Men excels;
For what's in Knowledge choice and rare
  But in his Breast securely dwells?

CHORUS.

His silent Breast and faithful Heart
Preserve the *Secrets* of the *Art*.

III.

From scorching Heat, and piercing Cold;
  From Beasts, whose Roar the Forest rends;
From the Assaults of Warriours bold
  The Masons' *Art* Mankind defends.

CHORUS.

Be to this *Art* due Honour paid,
From which Mankind receives such Aid.

IV.

Ensigns of State, that feed our Pride,
   Distinctions troublesome, and vain!
By Masons true are laid aside:
   Art's free-born Sons such Toys disdain.

CHORUS.

Ennobled by the *Name* they bear,
Distinguisht by the *Badge* they wear.

V.

Sweet Followship, from Envy free:
   Friendly Converse of Brotherhood;
The Lodge's lasting Cement be!
   Which has for Ages firmly stood.

CHORUS.

A Lodge thus built, for Ages past
Has lasted, and will ever last.

VI.

Then in our Songs be Justice done
   To those who have enrich'd the *Art*,
From JABAL down to Burlington,
   And let each Brother bear a Part.

CHORUS.

Let noble Masons' Healths go round:
Their Praise in lofty Lodge resound.

ENTER'D 'PRENTICE'S SONG.

BY OUR LATE BROTHER
MR. MATTHEW BIRKHEAD, DECEAS'D.

To be sung when all GRAVE BUSINESS *is over, and with the Master's leave.*

I.

Come, let us prepare,
We Brothers that are
Assembled on merry Occasion;
Let's drink, laugh, and sing;
Our Wine has a Spring:
Here's a Health to an Accepted Mason.

II.

The World is in pain
Our Secrets to gain,
And still let them wonder and gaze on;
They ne'er can divine
The *Word* or the *Sign*
Of a Free and an Accepted Mason.

III.

'Tis *This* and 'tis *That,*
They cannot tell *What,*
Why so many Great Men of the Nation
Should *Aprons* put on,
To make themselves one
With a Free and an Accepted Mason.

IV.

Great Kings, Dukes, and Lords,
Have laid by their Swords,
Our *Myst'ry* to put a good Grace on;

And ne'er been asham'd
To hear themselves nam'd
With a Free and an Accepted Mason.

v.

Antiquity's Pride
We have on our side,
And it maketh Men just in their Station:
There's nought but what's good
To be understood
By a Free and an Accepted Mason.

vi.

Then join *Hand in Hand,*
T' each other firm stand,
Let's be merry, and put a bright Face on.
What Mortal can boast
So Noble a Toast,
As a Free and an Accepted Mason?

It is thought not amiss to insert here a Paragraph from an old Record of Masons, viz. The Company of Masons, being otherwise termed Free Masons, of ancient Standing and good Reckoning, by means of affable and kind Meetings diverse Tymes, and as a loving Brotherhood showld use to doe, did frequent this mutual Assembly in the Tyme of King Henry V. the 12th Year of his most gracious Reign. And the said Record describing a Coat of Arms, much the same with that of the London Company of Freemen Masons, it is generally believ'd that the said Company is descended of the ancient Fraternity; and that in former Times no Man was made Free of that Company, until he was install'd in some Lodge of Free and Accepted Masons, as a necessary Qualification. But that laudable Practice seems to have been long in Dissuetude. The Brethren in foreign Parts have also discover'd that several noble and ancient Societies and Orders of Men have derived their *Charges and Regulations* from the Free Masons, (which are now the most ancient Order upon Earth,) and perhaps were originally all Members too of the said ancient and worshipful Fraternity. But this will more fully appear in due time.

LONDON, *this* 17*th Day of January*, 172$\frac{2}{3}$.

AT the *Quarterly Communication*, This Book, which was undertaken at the Command of His *Grace* the Duke of MONTAGU, our late **Grand-Master**, having been regularly approved in Manuscript by the *Grand-Lodge*, was this Day produced here in Print, and approved by the *Society:* Wherefore we do hereby Order the same to be Published, and recommend it for the Use of the *Lodges.*

PHILIP, DUKE of WHARTON, *Grand-Master.*
I. T. DESAGULIERS, *Deputy Grand-Master.*

FINIS.

ANALYTICAL INDEXES

TO

Anderson's Constitutions,

PREPARED BY

ALBERT G. MACKEY. M. D.

———◆———

I.

INDEX TO THE HISTORICAL PART.

A.

5*

II.

INDEX TO THE CONSTITUTIONAL PART.

THE END.

Sinews were all that remained of the curtain linings in the dining room, but the tired and heavy velvet fronts were intact, effective in concealing the world from Clair, and Clair from the world. They appeared as one solid swathe of burnt orange and were almost successful at keeping out daylight, except for a pale ragged line on the wall above. Slipping her hand in at exactly the right point to push one aside, a blinding pain caused her to let go again and the curtain fell shut. Oblivious to the dust that was now spinning around the room, she tried again, increasing the opening more gradually, one by one sliding the bodies of velvet along their yellowed tracks. Morning spilled in, reaching everywhere it could as she bunched the curtains around their waists securing each with a tightly twisted cord. She rested a hand on the cold window. Water fell from the ends of her fingers and raced to the sill where it merged into round puddles. Through the aperture she admired the tall evergreen tree, just as one dark arm began to nod and a sparkling of dew scattered. A collared dove had landed with little grace and cocked its head. As she smiled out at her visitor, the bird twitched mechanically, turning its black bead of an eye toward her.

The house in which Clair lived had gazed across a cobbled street for more than a hundred years. It stood shyly offset from a taller,

neater property. The occupant of the tall house was a well-ordered man who kept himself to himself. Clair sometimes gathered clues about him through a slightly opened door or an evening lit window. Once or twice in the seven years that he had lived there she had climbed his worn stone steps to post a misdirected letter, but, in truth, she didn't know Brian at all. She did, however, like him. His privacy and quiet presence stirred both a curiosity in her and a duty to look after him, albeit from a distance.

When an unfamiliar visitor approached the foot of the stone steps, she watched carefully. The man wore a square cut jacket and trousers the colour of envelopes. He had a brown peaked cap tilted slightly back on his round head. The man carried no parcel or packet. He did, however, have what appeared to be a very thin book tucked beneath his arm. The stranger took hold of the thick iron railing and hauled his body up each step then rapped the brass letterbox so hard that he sound ricocheted from house to house. After a few minutes, the door opened a little. The man stood quickly upright then waggled his fingers in the air; it struck Clair that he had no idea at all he was being watched. Through the narrow gap in the open door she could hardly see anything of Brian and could only hope that the visitor was not causing him any trouble. The light breeze carried their words in another direction, but to observe was adequate for the time being and also brought the added benefit of distracting her from the cold. She knew that her camera was in reach should she need it. The conversation between the two men lasted only a minute or two

4

and reached a simple finale when Brian took a piece of paper from the man and closed the door with a loud crack. The dove launched itself off the waving branch, forced its way up into the air and disappeared. Very quickly it was as if Brian, the man and the bird had never been there at all.

Clair sank into a sigh. She found comfort in Brian's brief appearance. It wasn't that she *needed* anyone in her life, but if she ever did she imagined Brian to be just the type of person she could depend on. A deep breath flowed over her lip and she considered brushing her teeth, but there was no rush; she had all day, longer if she wanted. Shaking open a cloth she cleared more condensation from the window and watched as the sill puddles grew. Damp air filled her nose. Breathing was easy, but the more she dwelled on the thought of it, the more cumbersome the process seemed to become. She began to visualise cauliflower lungs and a ruddy heart pumping thick blood around the network of her veins. 'I'll have to stop!' she mumbled to herself, trying instead to concentrate on the window.

Suddenly, she began to feel unwell, and, concerned she might suffer heart failure or that her blood cells might clump into a thrombotic clot, she decided to stop attending to the condensation. Her cold wet hand wiped across her thigh, leaving a dark spot on her jeans. Clair had never thought about it before, but began to wonder what the wiped glass looked like from the *outside*. The wiped smears and water trails, she feared, may look to a passer-by as if someone

were trapped, that the occupant were in some sort of difficulty, or worse. She might also have smeared a watery message saying 'help', or left handprints followed by dripping runs as her damaged body dropped to the floor, perhaps even have pulled down a curtain by grabbing onto it, or cracked a window in her moment of trauma. All were entirely possible.

'Are you all right? 'Someone get help!' came Brian's desperate shouts as he hammered severely on the door.

Shuddering at her own capacity for daydreaming, Clair urged herself to start getting ready and stop worrying about fantastical misfortunes. She passed through the icy hall and climbed the stairs to the bathroom to wash.

The dove returned to the quiet branch and turned its head to look for her.

'What a dreadful man!' Brian exclaimed as he locked the front door. 'Wasn't he *dreadful*?' he asked Boris, who had spent the morning sitting motionless in his old chair.
'Yes, he was' Brian answered to himself as he glanced across at the toothy black typewriter. It gaped back in a semi-smile, a stack of empty paper beside it. 'What do you think, Boris? Start now or after breakfast?'

The kitchen was his favourite morning workspace, and was equipped with far more than one person could ever need. Utensils stared up from a huge brown crock, their limbs crossing one another awkwardly, and knives for every purpose hid their sharpness in an angled block of pine. Against the wall were sleeping machines in shiny steel and behind the cupboard doors rested neatly aligned crockery. The polished kitchen seized him in its view, and as he held the round belly of the kettle in the line of tap water, he was watched by a thousand distorted versions of himself.

With just the right amount of water for one hot drink, he clunked the kettle onto the stove and sweet gas tinged his throat. With an Apostle spoon his mother had given him, he scooped powdery black tea into a small teapot and turned his eye to the fruit bowl. Apples, pears and dusty grapes tumbled romantically down one side, and, now that the bright morning sun beamed into the kitchen, strong shadows had formed in the gaps between the fruits, and stretched along the counter top. A scene of chiaroscuro distracted him completely and he darted from the kitchen to fetch his sketchpad from the dresser drawer. On the way he wafted Boris disturbing nothing more than a few fine hairs.

'I am going to eat later' he told Boris. 'I've got things I need to do.'

One blue eye nicked open before closing back to sleep. Boris was used to feeling the rush of a body around the place and human drama had stopped bothering him long ago. Nothing in the house bothered him any more, not even the kicking of the kettle as it began to approach a boil, and he carelessly drifted into another of his worlds.

Brian opened out the pad and unclipped the brass clasps on the pencil box. He breathed in the scent of cedar as he made the first grey sweeps across the paper, beginning with the wide arc of the bowl.

The white porcelain was dazzling as Clair swirled her hand in a figure of eight, blending the water as it dropped from the taps. Never in her life had she had to struggle for water, it was always *there*, ready to comfort, refresh, do whatever she demanded of it. The hard steel taps dug into her palms as she closed off the flow and, apart from a few harmonious drops, she was left with the simple soothe of lapping water and warm comfort spreading up her arms. Forming a two-handed cup beneath the water, she lifted the warmth to her face and let it spill over her closed eyes and mouth. Washing was a chore when she *thought* about it, but once she was doing it she found she enjoyed the process immensely. After three or four repetitions of the same washing motion, she opened her eyes and looked at herself in the mirror. The bluish strip-light gave a lifeless

tint to her skin. She inspected her rutted forehead, and then her eyes. Gossamers of red spread across the damp grey surface and into the corners. She never understood why the lines around people's eyes were referred to as *crow's feet* or *laughter lines* as neither matched their shape or their cause. *Grimace lines* or *pain lines* suited much better, she thought, but whatever the name there seemed to be more than there were yesterday. More white hairs on her jumbled head too, shining out like seams of quartz. Clair pulled at a strand and felt it prick as it pinged out of her scalp and fell invisibly to the floor. There were so many that she only attended to the haywire ones.

She drifted irrepressibly into her reflection. It was definitely her, but the gap between who she felt she was and what she looked like in the mirror seemed to widen every day.

A deep searching of her face used up immeasurable time, enough to cool the water in the basin and cause the muscles in her hands and arms to ache.

'When did you get this *old*?' She asked aloud, as the search drained away with the water, and she patted a coarse towel over her skin.

Clean and dressed, breakfast would normally have been next, but the glow of the sun stopped her in her tracks. Everything on the dining room table had become suddenly super-impressive: keys

bunched together with scarlet string; a paper-knife; a pile of striped tea towels; a purple comb; some books, yesterday's teacup, and a red apple that looked almost too real to eat. To anyone else it was clutter, but to Clair it was beautiful and she took her cold camera carefully in her hands. The black lens stared blankly as she gently brushed away a few minor specks of dust then turned the camera's dark eye toward the table. A wink of yellow confirmed there was a film inside and she pulled the winding lever with her thumb. The mechanical clicking that emitted from the camera nourished more than breakfast. The light, the shadow, the colours, the shapes and the positioning of the objects on the table, everything had come together decisively with the light and looked *right*.

No longer could she feel the steel camera back pressed hard against her cheek, or her heart drumming in her chest. Most of Clair and most of the world had disappeared completely.

She had bound the scene. It was hers.

The apples had placed themselves in the forefront of Brian's attention leaving the pears to fade into his mental background. The decision to put art before food was a regret now that hunger griped. He had no idea how much time he had passed up and was quite disappointed with his creative efforts. Even Boris had long since had

a wash and gone out, leaving nothing but a hint of himself. Upset, Brian considered screwing the drawing up into a ball but instead he breathed deeply and persisted, impatiently throwing loose lines and liberally shading the paper. It was turning out to be an unsatisfactory morning and his temples were beginning to ache from concentration, frustration, and a deficiency of sugar. Eventually, he decided that enough was enough and grated back the chair, scraping his annoyance along the floor tiles. He stood, flashed open his hands and cracked his fingers, removing the stiffness that the tight hold on the pencils gave.

Fully upright, he looked down at the drawing and, with a raised eyebrow, accepted that it looked far better with a little distance.

'I'm quite pleased with that!'.

In reward, he plucked an apple from the bowl. Disturbing one of the soft pears, it landed with a light thud on the table then settled and a bruise began to form. He bit the fruit and a small cloudy drop of juice ran down his chin, spotting his crisp blue shirt. He suppressed a minor curse and wiped away the spot not noticing the yellow-jacketed wasp that had found its way in through a small hole under the door.

'Got it!'

The shutter ticked and Clair felt a small rush of contentment, as if someone, just for a second, had guaranteed that everything was

going to be all right. Unpredictably motivated she began to prowl the room until the curve of a figurine hooked her. Despite a fine coating of dust, its smooth auburn wood caught the light in such a way that an abstract and gentle line was formed along its neck and body. She didn't need to see the rest of it; the curve alone was rich and worthy of a frame. It was a detail she would not have noticed had she not been looking through the camera.

'That's good,' she said aloud, and shot it.

Then, through the window, she shot a bird on the tree; a fat ball of grey with its head tucked into its wing. After three or four more impulsive takes, and a brief pang of concern for the bird, the last frame was used and the film had creaked to a halt inside the camera. Satisfied, she pushed the button into the recess underneath and wound the film squealing back into its canister. Opening up the black cavity, she plucked out the film and dropped it into the drawer where it landed among a hoard of others.

'A successful morning', she grinned, replacing the camera in its bag. It didn't matter that she might never see the images made, she had enjoyed the *photographing*; that was the most important part and a warm satisfaction had wrapped itself around her. Far too absorbed in the flow of photography, she hadn't noticed the clacking of shoes along the path to her front door. The bite of the metal letterbox shattered her fragile contentment, as did the subsequent slap of a

thick envelope touching down on the peeling doormat.

'Hello?'

With no one to give an answer she opened the door to look, closing it again when the coldness bound her ankles. She reached for the packet, the smell of autumn exuding from the brown paper. Its back had been securely taped, and the front displayed her address written neatly and completely in black. Warily, she pressed around the packet's shape. Along the edge, past a bright line of stamps, her fingers discovered a stepped texture, and unable to withhold curiosity any longer, she delicately peeled off the tape. As she opened the envelope, a generous bundle of photographs revealed itself, bound together by two fraught elastic bands. Tucked in the front was a written paper note.

It read, simply, 'Thinking of you'.

'Thinking of you? Who's thinking of *me*?'

Clair plucked out the note and turned it over, hoping for more information. There was nothing on the back. She looked again at the envelope in case she had missed something, but even the postmark held no clues, having been smudged to illegibility.

The twisted rubber bands tutted as she rolled off them onto the table where they relaxed into overlapping circles. As the contents of the packet began to separate in her hands, an indiscernible aroma stung the insides of her nose; fading menthol, rot, or some kind of chemical, she was not sure. Before the chains of her imagination could link the smell to poison or contamination, Clair was suddenly and uncontrollably drawn to another place, absorbed completely and utterly by the dark-eyed gaze of a tall man. He was about twenty or twenty-five, and wore a happy grin and slicked back hair.

'Who is *that*?' questioned Clair, though she already felt a glimmer of recognition.

The reverse of the photograph was void of any specifics, but on it she found another message scribbled in pencil;

'To Clair, love Dad'.

'Get out!' Brian yelled as he felt a stab in his ankle. He picked up the sketchpad from the table and waved the grey apples and pears at the wasp, swiping like a bat to a tennis ball until the wasp was knocked dazed onto the floor.

'Evil thing!'

14

The wasp stumbled to its feet. Unable to see anything at all, it walked a few unsteady paces then stopped, the pain in its back unbearable. Two or three short attempts to fly followed but only a futile whirring could be managed. In darkness, the wasp held still. A moment or two later it braced its body and tried again. Before it had an opportunity to make even the smallest lift, its small mouth filled with acridity and tiny body began to blister. It could do nothing but writhe and curl. Whiteness wrapped around the wasp's body and tightened until it could feel nothing.

'Ugh,' Brian said repugnantly, and pressed open the bin.

He dropped the tissue into it then swept his hand across the drawing, as if wiping it clean. The small puncture wound on his leg pulsed with anger.

Clair's body hit back into the chair, kicking her backward and throwing her forward again; the *punctum* as forceful as a car crash.

'It can't be. Not Dad'

She urgently turned the image over and rechecked the handwriting. A small sense of relief passed through her as she noticed the neat writing on the note was different from the scrawl on the back of the photograph. Feeling foolish for thinking that her father might have written to her from beyond the grave, she had suddenly generated a host of unanswered questions:

Who had written the note? Who had addressed the envelope? Who had delivered it? Why had her father written a message on the reverse of a photograph that was taken long before she had even been thought of?

All Clair ever wanted was for life to be predictable and uncomplicated; she hadn't anticipated anonymous deliveries and, even though she had dispelled her initial, irrational fear, the situation filled her with anxiety. As she stared at the image and her father stared back, an inner sickness rose through her feet and legs, spreading quickly to her chest. Her heart changed rhythm. With deep breaths she fought against the familiar symptoms that could stamp out a whole week of time, and, gradually, the frightful panic began to subside. She sipped her sugary tea and stared wide-eyed at the bundle. Despite her dread, she gave herself no option but to look at each of the photographs in turn, and, like tarot cards, she cautiously dispensed each one with her shaking hand, taking in details from each. One by one, each of the pictures stole her attention, pushing her between intrigue and repugnancy. Her earlier, pleasurable photography session might as well have never taken place. Now she was hostage, and disallowed from looking at anything else in the room.

Slowly, she constructed a grid on the table.

'It's only paper,' she reminded herself.

16

Before her were squares and rectangles of varying sizes, some black and white, and others washed out colour, unsurprising given their age and poor quality. Among the colour snapshots was a shirtless man sitting on the low steps of a caravan; a group of young adults posing beside a lake with bicycles; and a fair-haired girl sitting beside a headless man on the beach. This was surely Clair and her father.

'I'd completely forgotten about that', muttered Clair as she studied the four-inch picture. She guessed that she was about five years old when the snapshot had been taken, and assumed, like most of the family photographs, her mother had taken it. In it, she was wearing what she seemed to recall was a favourite t-shirt and though her eyes were not smiling, her face was young and bright. Her father's tall body towered beside the rock. It was cut off at the neck and underlined her with a long dark shadow. To anyone else, the image would be viewed as an amateur beach snapshot, one that would quite normally be placed in a flip album with donkey rides and ice-lolly faces. For Clair, the recollections were not of leisure or pleasure. Instead the long forgotten childhood experience of sitting on a seaside rock had trailed to numerous other details from well outside of the frame. In her mind, she could see a wicker picnic hamper with green plates, taste warm sandwiches, and feel the fear of a punishment that hadn't yet taken place. It terrified her to think that so much information from her childhood was still there, lodged in her bones and tissue only to burst out again when she least

expected.   This one photograph marooned her in another time until she had become completely unthinking of anything but the past.

As she drifted, something unexpected happened that ran to her core.   Out of nowhere, she *heard* her father's voice.   The words were indistinguishable, but the stern and shouting tone was definitely him. Panic scalded her face like boiling water.   Feeling that he may appear at any moment and admonish her for being so stupid, she slammed the picture on the table face down.   Breathing hard, she held it firm, until the sudden stab of a ringing telephone lifted her out of the chair.

'Who is it?' she barked into the receiver, and turned to look for something visually soothing.

'Miss Bodmin?'

'Yes?,' she snapped.

'It's Brian. From across the road.'

Heated panic turned to a shiver of relief that ran down from the top of her scalp through her face, neck and chest before ending in her legs.   Her skin broke into tiny bumps, and she took an audible in-breath.

'Brian! How are you?'

Her voice had softened to politeness, but was still quickened and shaky.

'I am fine. Are you busy with something?' he continued. 'I can call you back. It's just that I need to talk to you about the tree.' 'The tree? Why? What's wrong with it?'

'I have told you already, Miss Bodmin,' he replied in a disgruntled voice. 'It is casting a shadow right across my front. It's grown so much this year. When will you be cutting it down?'

Clair stretched out the coils of the telephone cable and twisted her body to look through the window. The glass was much clearer of condensation since everything had warmed a little. 'We talked about it last year,' he continued, 'and the year before. You said you'd do it then. It isn't fair, Miss Bodmin. Really, it isn't.'

She admired the majestic height and breadth of the dark conifer that she had watched develop through her life, always enjoying both its presence and the birdlife that it attracted. It felt somehow like a friend.

'It looks healthy to me, Brian' she reasoned, vaguely recalling the conversation. Despite it being a radical subject, she was quite thankful to be discussing it at that very moment.

'There's no point looking at it *now*, Miss Bodmin. Look at it later and you'll see what I mean. Not only is it blocking *my* light but those awful birds are driving me mad. I am trying to work.' 'The doves?' Clair queried.

'Doves, pigeons, *rats of the sky*' he scorned.

At that moment one dove, then another, and another, arrived in the tree as if wanting to join the debate. Before long the three of them were purring loudly at differing rates.

'They're lovely birds, Brian, they chatter to me every day!'

'Are you *mad* Miss Bodmin?' he retorted sharply. 'They are *birds.* You cannot have a conversation with a bird. They are not even attractive. They aren't song thrushes or goldfinches, are they?,' he rambled on with increasing acidity. 'Please get rid of that spiky thing and plant a nicer tree. Somewhere else, so I can have my sun back.'

Clair wanted to defend the tree, to explain that she had often seen small birds sheltering and eating there, even a siskin once or twice, but disapproval had crept in like a cat. She did not want to cut the tree down, and, torn between upsetting either Brian or the birds, she opted for deferral.

'I'll have a look this afternoon, when the sun moves round' she suggested. 'Can I call you back?'

'Please do.'

Clair wondered what had bitten him; he wasn't usually so abrupt.

'Oh, and Brian, I wondered ...' Clair continued, 'who was the man that came to your door this morning, the man in the brown uniform? Is there anything I need to know?'

'No, Miss Bodmin. Nothing for you to worry about.'

'But the paper? Will I be getting one?'

'I have to go. Ring me later.' There was a click, and an empty, humming tone.

'Goodbye Brian,' Clair mumbled at half volume. Then, before she even had time to finish her sigh she remembered the photographs.

The tip of the tall tree swayed a little, assured by the chill of the autumn air and the gentle weight of the birds that worked and rested in its secretive foliage. Despite vast differences in size and surface the inhabitants tolerated one another well. Other creatures scratched and crawled there, maintaining its bark, relieving it of itch and infestation in return for shelter. Unbeknown to any other living thing, the tree breathed very slowly and contentedly as the sap moved about its veins. With a slow push, it stretched out a fine threadlike root beneath the nearby houses.

Brian didn't like to cut people off, but there were times when a little abruptness was necessary in order to get things done. The huge and ugly tree was a blot on his view and he could not help but look at it each time he passed by the window. His sketchpad had

folded back on itself in the commotion and was slightly crumpled at one corner. Its textured whiteness was also dotted with a tiny yellow speckle from the impact of the wasp.

'Women!' Brian exclaimed, before adding 'and wasps!'

Boris ignored him, unimpressed. Brian's lower leg throbbed as a weal formed like a drop of honey, surrounded by a heated red circle. His motivation to draw had diminished and instead he dragged out the twisted chair he had made one slow and rainy day, hauling it in to reach the typewriter. He looked at Boris whose slothful approach to life populated a whole new article in Brian's mind, and an outpouring of black words began about the sheer laziness of the domestic cat.

Boris turned and faced the other way.

Now that the day was entirely tangled, Clair considered carefully which thread she should follow next. The tree wasn't urgent and could be forgotten about until later, and there were things to do in the house that could also wait, but the photographs would not go away and she knew she must attend to them. Putting them into an album was an option, but they wouldn't mean anything to anyone else in the future. Perhaps she would put them in a drawer, pretend they had never arrived at all, but that carried a fear that they would jump out at her again and prompt even more

memories that she did not want. Even throwing them away posed a problem, as they would rest in the bin until next Monday when the bin men came, in which time she might have changed her mind and taken them out again.

She took hold of a black and white photograph and inspected it. It was the image of a future-father, a man who knew nothing of raising a family; independent, with dark eyes and black carefree hair. Here was a man who looked a little like Clair in her 20s. A man who was dead.

She placed him into her palm, and, for a moment or two this tiny version of a human being amused her. Like the giant in a fairy tale, she felt a satisfying power flood through her and, for once, in control. A short line popped into her mind from a story she once read.

'Come closer so I can see you better,' said the king, who was thrilled to be king over someone at last.' *

She studied the details of the figure thinner than her little finger. He wore dark shiny boots and trousers smartly creased along their length, a white shirt, and a bow tie of which colour she had no idea. The dash of a white cigarette between his fingers conjured the strong smell of nicotine stained hands that she had known throughout her childhood.

As she studied him, a strange sensation spread through her hand. Like a delicate tickle at first, quickly it grew into a burning itch, as if her skin was reacting to the paper itself. As the itch crept towards the blue veins in her wrist, she wondered if the spirit of her father was seeping into her skin. She told herself she was being stupid, that a dead man's dark past bleeding from a photograph was a ridiculous notion, and her hand responded by spontaneously closing up. Without thinking, she had screwed up her father into a crumpled heap. As her fingers relaxed again, the paper began to unfold. With gradual, uneasy movements, it made slight sounds of discontent as it attempted to regain its flatness. Then, eerily, it stopped. Immediately Clair felt driven to dispose of it, to destroy it entirely just in case she may be infused with even the smallest amount of wickedness. Her father already looked misshapen with heavy creases, but not content with this and determined to mitigate any further risk to herself, she decided to tear the picture up, to put an end to whatever dangers it may contain.

She nicked the middle of the top edge and pulled at the paper, forcing an untidy tear. It wasn't easy to break into, but once she had begun it took minimal effort to tear right through her father's face, down through his suit, to the wooden planks beneath his shoes. Clair then placed the two spoiled halves on the table side by side with a void between them.

'Where his heart should have been', she thought.

Still not content that the feeling was resolved, she removed some small, sharp scissors from a tin on the dresser and began to cut

24

fiercely, the metal warming her skin as she worked. Ignoring the potential of a blister, she continued until she had a heap of tiny abstract shapes; a piece of coat, a smiling cheek, a seamed pocket, slices of sky; rough edged areas of grey. She found she could rearrange the pieces into disjointed scenes, like the sliding tile puzzles she had as a child, but regardless of the comedy potential of mixing up a person, her memories continued to form. Determined to rid herself, Clair replaced the scissors and took out of the drawer a small box of matches.

The burning on his leg was becoming unbearable, and, cursing the dead wasp, Brian dabbed some cream from a bent metal tube onto the sting. It quietened right away and, less irritated, he straightened his trouser leg. Catching a glimpse of his face in the round bathroom mirror he tracked a hand up his neck. Tiny black hairs pricked him like pins and he felt that a visit to the barbers would soon be necessary, but, with work now pressing, returned to his desk and continued to hammer out more words. Line by line, a story grew and as he thought about how to conclude it he stopped to grumble to Boris.

'I wish you could catch wasps. I wish you could catch anything.'

Boris reached out his legs and extended his piercing pink claws. His eyes extended into a smile, and he began a methodical purr. He

had learned to enjoy the feeling in his ears that human sounds gave him and knew that food that seemed to come frequently with them.

He hadn't needed to kill anything for months.

Ashes remained in the grate but Clair decided to proceed without emptying out the last fire. She smoothed out a page from a month-old newspaper and folded it, turning up the sides to make a flat paper tray. Into it, she dropped the jumbled grey pieces of her father. The newsprint was, by chance, an old article about divorce that she had chosen not to read when the paper was new and, ignoring the words for a second time, she lifted the container with both hands and placed it onto the black iron grate. Adding a nibble of firelighter, she took out a match and cracked its head. The flame caught right away and the paper began to pucker. Wisps of grey smoke curled into the dark hole of the chimney and out into the sky.

With the first burning quickly over, there were several other versions of the man still on the table and Clair considered whether to incinerate them one by one, or to make a big fire for the lot. 'Maybe I am supposed to do something with the ashes' she thought, wondering whether there were any protocols for burning photographs of dead parents.

She rose to her feet, rubbing a sore knee. The arrangement of the photographs continued to mangle her memories, confusing everything. Some recollections began as happy ones, like the forest walk, which Clair had enjoyed, but then an inevitable darkness pulled a cloud across. When the smallest good memory did start to glimmer, she couldn't help but wonder if she should keep just one of the photographs, maybe even two.

Undecided, she opened a window and let in a roll of fresh air. The visiting doves were looking in, tilting their heads in puzzlement.

'Lucky you', she said to them. 'You don't ever have to think about photographs'.

Across the road she noticed Brian was opening his window, too.

'Maybe he's burning the family album as well!' she joked to herself.

He slammed the window shut with a bang.

'If I had a gun I'd shoot you all,' groaned Brian as the gathering of doves grew, added to by the arrival of some noisy crows. 'How am I supposed to work with all that racket?'

It wasn't that he could even hear them very much from the back of the house, but he was feeling agitated as the wasp sting had begun to aggravate even more than before. The cat was useless, the tree was

out of control, and he had far too much work to be getting on with. It was not a good day. He went back to the desk and began clattering fiercely on the typewriter. It was a wonder he could hear anything else at all as he concentrated on the last few paragraphs, unaware of his own frowning eyebrows and tightly pursed lips.

'You really *are* quite beautiful,' said Clair admiring the sleek grey birds as they crooned to one another. She didn't mind the raucous black crows either; to Clair they were another part of the natural colloquy that tumbled in on the cool air. She breathed the pleasantness into her throat, cleansing away the irritants of stale, burning paper and paraffin. She had only made a small amount of progress and, even when looking out of the window for distractions, could not forget that the tiny men waited in rows behind her like a Lilliputian army poised to attack. Even after the first burning she still wasn't sure she would succeed in ridding herself, and wondered if she would ever be able to lighten herself again from the weight of the reopened memories.

'If only you hadn't *thought* of me,' she muttered, without knowing to whom the complaint was directed.

Then the air brought with it a fresh idea.

Clair sometimes took photographs of *things*, often before squirrelling them away somewhere in the house, or before discarding an object that was completely beyond repair. It didn't matter what

the object was, a pair of broken shoes or a collar from her long-deceased dog; she found that photographing something stopped her needing to think about. It was as if the camera sucked up the loss on her behalf and, with the click of a button, she was shielded from the symptoms of grief. She considered whether the same approach might work in this situation, but with the realisation that past things could still find a route back into her thoughts, she was faced with a new anxiety. She loosened her tight neckline with her fingers, then, feeling she had nothing she could lose, took out her camera again and produced from a pocket a new roll of film. Loaded quickly and expertly, she wound it to the first frame. Insecurity led her to put the camera strap around her neck, feeling the uncomfortably wide band both pulling and comforting at the same time, and she stood on the dining chair, a loud creak adding to her unease. The room was adequately lit by the bright day, and she trained the lens on the battalion before her. Unable to fit them all into one frame, she thought about moving them to the floor but this would be far too much effort. She concluded that it didn't really matter whether they were in focus or not; this was simply an exercise in eradication.

The shutter button ticked. She shifted to the right, wound on, and it ticked again. And again. Now the cremation could take place.

The lifeless body of the wasp was pressed down into the depth of the bin under fruit skins and plastic wrapping, its short life already forgotten. Apart from the tiny dot in Brian's sketchpad, the only other suggestion of its existence was the lesion on his lower leg. He found it a struggle not to scratch, but had moved beyond grumbling about it.

The neat front room was beginning to gain afternoon sunrays, and with his article now complete, he made a quick lunch before taking up his pencils again; a plate of oily sardines laid out neatly on a slab of toast. He remembered the huge shadow that would soon be creeping across the window, and also that Clair hadn't yet bothered to call. Frustration took over and he pushed the plate aside. From her open window he assumed her to be home and slipping his feet into a pair of polished shoes, he left the house and crossed the road, glaring at the monstrous evergreen. The sheen on his new shoes looked quite out of place on Clair's path as the damp, dark and downward slope led him to feel like he were taking a trip into the underground. His knuckles made a deadened sound on the old wet door and he twitched in displeasure. With folded arms, he looked around at the scattered green mosses that had curled away from the roof, and listened carefully for sounds of movement from inside the house. Clair held still, nervous that there may be more unexpected packets to come, more dead relatives. When everything was quiet and she felt sure that nothing untoward was about to happen, she picked up the next photograph in the line. It had been snapped

during a summer camping trip, one she did not remember, but one that instantly joined the failed ranking of every other expedition she had been on with her father. Just the thought of those trips prompted nausea and with blatant rejection of any finer details, she took another matchstick from the yellow box.

Muffled knocking stopped her, and, cautiously, she made her way into the hall. With the photo and box of matches in one hand, she turned the door handle with the other and peered through a thin gap to the outside.

When a grey face slowly revealed itself Brian wondered if it *was* Clair. Deep lines dug across her forehead and around her eyes, as if she had not slept for days. As the opening widened, any minor concern was soon replaced by an all-consuming frustration as he remembered the purpose of his visit.

'Miss Bodmin. Can I come in?' he asked importantly.

Before she had time to think of a reason why not, or to construct an apology for her untidiness, he had placed himself inside the musty hall where each saccade took in a separate detail; the frayed collar of a hanging coat, dust on a picture frame, a barometer that pointed to 'change', then a small black and white photograph in Clair's hand.

'Oh! Are you looking at photographs?' Brian asked with a sudden interest.

'No,' Clair replied, 'I'm burning them,' her voice flat with honesty.

Brian laughed, expecting her to laugh back, but her flint face indicated that she wasn't joking at all. The feint smell of burnt paper and paraffin wafted into the hall, and his eyes and mouth widened into dismay.

'You can't *burn* photographs!' he bellowed, striding boldly into the dining room as if she were a tenant in his house.

Clair wanted to explain her reasons but he had already passed by her in a whisk of cold air and was standing over the table looking at the lines of images laid out for incineration. She followed him, rather perturbed by his over-emotional response. She was, however, used to her own way of things inside her own house and reached over the grate striking another match. Flames licked the corner of the tent and spread along the guy rope, then up her father's leg.

'Stop it! Please! Stop it! *You can't burn photographs!*' he repeated.

His distress bemused Clair.

'Why not?' she asked. 'They're no use to me.'

'Why *not*?' He echoed. 'Because they are *people*! That's why not.

Look, this man, and this little girl. *Real* people, Miss Bodmin! How could you even *think* of doing such a thing?'

He held up the very first photograph his hand met with, pinching it tightly between thumb and finger so as not to let it fall. Without even looking at its content he continued.

'Miss Bodmin. Please have some respect.' Then he put the image back onto the table and randomly picked another. 'Look at this little girl. Surely you can't burn *her*! Don't you have any idea how important these pictures are?'

'Important? Why?'

'Because they *are*!' Exasperated, he continued with his defence. 'They are our social history! They must be looked after, protected!'

The pitch of Brian's voice was climbing higher, reverberating around the clutter in the room, and passionate tears began to line his eyes. Clair would rather have listened to the crows and didn't understand his alarm at all. To her the photographs - *all* photographs - were bits of paper loaded with unwanted remembrances.

The pair looked at one another until Clair calmly broke the pause.

'The little girl is me, Brian,' she retorted, dryly, 'and that man is my father. I can burn us both if I want to.'

Brian's mouth crumpled. He perused her face but her indifference worked him up even more and blood spilled into his cheeks. Clair was suddenly captivated, not by his raging attractiveness, or his powerful defence of the photograph as an historical object, but by the dramatic contrast between the redness of his face and the blueness of his shirt.

'Miss Bodmin. Really! Why would you do that?' Then suspicion lowered his tone to mistrust. 'Are you doing some sort of ritual here? Is that what this is?'

'There is nothing sinister here, I can assure you,' she replied, shaken that he had even conceived such a possibility. 'I simply don't want to be reminded of the past, that's all. Photographs are terrible for that.'

'Then I'll have them if you are only going to burn them,' he continued, and began to gather up the photographs. His outrage was peppered with sad thoughts of his own father who he missed so painfully.

'By all means,' Clair replied. 'You can have the memories that go with them too. Take the lot.'

Like an undisciplined child, Brian stamped out of the house, clumsily followed by Clair who did not understand any of the fuss.

'They're just bits of paper', she muttered, half hoping that he hadn't heard.

'There are *souls* in these bits of paper,' he yelled back.

The gate slammed shut, full-stopping on his last word and rattling loose the pitted metal catch. He crossed the road grasping the photographs tightly and slammed his front door just as hard.

The human was back. Boris quickly licked away the last of the shiny sardine oil. His belly was satisfied and his body wanted to sleep, but with an empty slice of toast left on the plate, the human was sure to bark at him. The cat flap huffed as he slipped through it and disappeared into the evening air.

The photographs had only been present for a matter of hours, but already the table looked bare without them and Clair wondered if she was missing the company of familial eyes or if it was to be a simple case of readjustment. Unsure, she felt slight relief that she had at least photographed them before letting them go. The sun had tracked across the sky and beamed into the kitchen leaving the

dining room chilly and damp. As she thudded the window shut, she noticed the pointed shadow of the tree running across the street like a crooked arrow, pointing to Brian's living room window. Her hand took up the telephone receiver and she dialed his number, but dropped it back down. Sensibly, she decided to wait until his anger had subsided.

At the table she stared nowhere, enjoying a moment of calm in what was turning out to be a perplexing day. The skin around her eyes felt as if she had been sobbing, but she had not shed a single tear. Then, just as she was beginning to relax again, the words 'Thinking of you' caught her attention. The square of paper stood to the left of the ticking clock, in the holding area for things that didn't yet have a process. As the note raised its voice louder, she knew she must do *something* with it.

With tender delicacy, as if handling a collection of fine and valuable artefacts, Brian picked the photographs one by one from the pile, placing them beside one another in neatly aligned rows. By the time he had finished laying them out, there was barely any room beside the typewriter; but, unbothered by the encroachment, he puffed at having saved them from a fate of ashes. Some of the images did look like Clair in her younger days and he accepted that some were of her father. Others, he thought, were probably uncles, aunts, cousins.

36

His index finger swayed through the air as if an unknown force would land his hand upon one, and he picked one out at random of a man leaning on a white railing with a dark haired girl and a small boy, and a calm grey sea behind. As he touched the paper, his finger seemed to warm slightly. It was a pleasant sensation, and he wondered if he could somehow have connected with the spirits within it. Drawn to protecting them, he left them on the desk to search for a suitable book or box to keep them in.

The unblinking faces stared out, waiting for him to return.

A white animal shot like a ghoul over the top of the wall, almost tripping Clair as it lurched and hid under the tree. She pulled her jacket tightly around her and spun around to see where the creature had gone. As she did, the 'thinking of you' note spiralled out of her hand and was caught on the breeze. She could do nothing but watch as it turned three choreographed circles. Despite taking larger than normal strides, trying rather comically to stamp on it, the note meandered along the road, and rested at the bottom of Brian's steps, as if knowing exactly where it was to go. She picked it up and brushed it clean of dirt before pushing it to tumble through the letterbox into the warmth. Clair turned to home, satisfied that the entire consignment was now nothing more to do with her. A man on

an aged bicycle passed her, his wheel hubs squeaking like guinea pigs with every turn.

'Evening,' the man said, without even looking at Clair.

'Hello' said Clair, charily.

'Been a nice day' the man said after he had passed by, hubs and voice tapering with each word. 'Cold tonight, though.'

'Yes' said Clair, relieved that the man was about to turn the corner. She shuddered.

The gate remained ajar, unable to shut since the catch had been so badly loosened. Inside the dark house and still with her coat on, Clair picked up the telephone and pressed the sequence of numbers for Brian, thinking it best to let him know that she had posted the note through. She also wanted to tell him that she had almost lost it in the wind, and that, instead of letting it go, had saved it for him.

The telephone pleaded but there was no reply. She tweaked the curtain edge and looked across the street. She thought she could see a figure in blue by the window.

As Brian drew the curtains to a close he saw movement at Clair's house and, just for a second, wondered what she might be doing. Then, without the outside world to worry about any more, he set about finishing his supper, collecting every last red drop of

tomato soup with the soft white bread. The food had been quite enjoyable, once he had overcome the initial annoyance of finding that both his sardines and Boris had disappeared.

Feeling heavy, he fought sluggishness, and, not wanting to waste the remainder of the day, returned to the photographs.

'Come on,' he muttered, urging himself to continue. 'Through hard work to the stars.' He had no idea where the saying came from but his father had often used it, and it always worked in pulling him up out of the chair.

The collection was now laid out across the dining room table along with an empty album he had found in a cupboard, its thick green leaves yearning to be filled. Disappointingly, he could not recall exactly his ideas from earlier, and began sliding the photographs around one another, changing their sequence. He was determined to find a narrative that was rational, believable. Some photographs were easier to place than others; the small black and white squares were clearly of an era before the colour prints, but, aside from technological differences, a system was not immediately clear. He found he had to make decisions on behalf of the subjects; not an easy thing to do. After some time, he was pleased to have created what he felt was a feasible timeline; he had built an entire family story. He began peeling the triangular backs from adhesive corners to trap each image irrevocably in the book. Strong glue

gripped them to the pages as tightly as Brian clung to the biography he had spent his evening inventing.

Boris flopped in and curled on the chair, exhausted, and the sound of his entrance prompted Brian to look at the clock. 'It is later than I thought!' he said and closed the book so that the faces inside pressed close against one another.

Hosts of invisible spiders strung silver threads around the tree like early Christmas swags. Beneath the branches a speckled thrush cracked a yellow snail shell with full force against a stone. It tipped its head to cast a slick eye downwards in between each strike, assessing its progress as hunger griped in its tiny stomach. Inside the beaten shell the snail lay prepared. During the night there had been so many births and deaths. Now, white stars were turning out one by one and the sky was changing from blue-black to pink, and then to winter gold.

Some mornings, Clair didn't really know what she was going outside for. Sometimes, she would be in need of a pint of milk, a loaf of bread or some firelighters, but occasionally she set out to experience the world in which other people seemed to buzz and thrive. Her mind flipped between envying those who could be a part

of all it so easily, and feeling very relieved that she was on the outside looking in.

It seemed that every time she walked along the road another outbuilding had appeared or another 'For Sale' sign had been hammered into the ground. Time seemed to move much faster outside her little house than in. She turned the corner, following the curve of iron railings on which an ever-present pair of leather gloves pointed fingers to the sky. As she neared the town, the rumbling traffic shook her. A square bus hissed, tipping people onto the pavement and suddenly she was in the hustle of shoppers and workers. Men joked loudly with one another from one side of the street to the other; people paced, hiding their faces behind loops of fur, some tilted so far forwards that Clair wondered how they could see anything but the pavement. Black dogs passed in opposite directions; and fumes curled into prams. She pulled her scarf up over the lower half of her face, not enjoying the exposure, but as the bodies moved by, Clair had the distinct feeling that no one could see her at all, that she was an invisible entity drifting inadvertently along. Even in direct faces, eyes seemed to stare beyond her, and she found herself uncomfortably gathering pace, her breath becoming almost as hard as the faces she observed.

Moving closer to the buildings, she placed herself in the shadows. Every now and then, in quickened steps, she caught a glimpse of a figure, a ghostly woman, who followed her through the

streets. Clair wondered who the woman was, then realised that the dark shape in the windows and bus stops belonged to her. The gentlest of characters, the years of anxiety pressed on her face meant every flicker of herself was a betrayal. Perhaps, she thought, it was *best* that no one could see her.

Oblivious of her existence, geese chanted their way across the sky and she looked up in admiration as they made their connected journey, communicating to one another constantly. Her attention turned to one bird in particular. It seemed to flap to its own rhythm entirely, floating separately amid the central void.

Eventually, the cold pushed Clair into a newspaper shop, and the heavy glass closed behind her. A little dazed, she stood still for a moment not knowing where to rest her eyes. Warmth came to her face.

'Can I help you?'

A man in a white woolen jumper glanced up from his work and welcomed her with a smile.

'He can *see* me!' she blushed as she whispered under her breath. Clair took hold of the first newspaper she touched and dropped it onto the counter.

'Fifty pence, my darling', said the man and stopped bundling papers while he waited for payment. Clair patted her cold hand around her pocket in search of coins, which she set flat on the counter.

'Thank you.' He threw the coin into the till where it fell awkwardly among the others. Clair wanted to start some idle chitchat about the weather, the traffic, Christmas - anything at all, but all words jammed firmly in her throat. With a partial smile, she turned and left the shop, the rolled newspaper shoved into her bag.

Directionless, the painted iron gates of Festival Park drew her in. Some of her childhood days had been spent there, but now the park was more for dogs and loners than families. Occasionally she saw a tired detail, the broken stone sundial or a flaking iron bench-end, which led her to remember small things. As if someone were flicking through channels on a TV set, a split second of her memory would come and go. Mother. Father. The good days. The bad.

A grey man caught Clair's attention. He stood raised slightly on a clod of ground and was addressing a group of twenty or so straight-faced others who listened intently. She half-wanted to slip unnoticed into the group and find out what the speech was about. Had she been truly invisible, she would have done so without question. Instead, she imagined the situation and concluded that, were she to be seen sneaking in, she would not be able to explain herself. Instead, she found a seat and wiped the dew from it with the

sleeve of her coat. Committed to staying there, at least for a little while, she was irritated by the lingering presence of the group, and took out her newspaper to shake them out of sight.

The reported world opened abruptly, and far away places unfolded. Clair searched for something relevant and gentle. When a large colour photograph seized her, she didn't see the old stray dog that trotted solidly past or the blackbird that hopped close beside her. Instead, she saw a mass of people somewhere in the world in the middle of a crisis. Bags and shoes were lost in commotion, and terror was scribed in their faces. In the foreground of the image was a young woman with a baby. One tiny thin arm with spindly fingers reached out. Behind her, an older woman streamed with tears. Another had a trickle of red coming from the top of her head down over her cheek. Shaken, Clair quickly shut the newspaper and tried to erase the image from her mind. She hoped the women had reached safety, but the tiny hand reaching out seemed etched into her   mind.
'How can I *un-see* this now?' she asked herself. 'I don't want to *know*'. Her despairing heart thudded.

She wondered if the men by the tree had also seen the news; perhaps that was what they were talking so seriously about. Castigating herself for having bought a newspaper in the first place she set off toward the gates, dropping the sadness of the world into the first available bin. She looked around at the trees for a moment, and up at the sky, trying hard to cleanse her mind. Hollowness

griped her insides. It was not morning hunger, but rather the feeling that a large 'something' in her was missing.

The skit of a grey squirrel in the grass brought amusement. Brian had already seen a kestrel hanging in the sky above a patch of rough grass on East Street. His morning walk was enjoyable and he felt pleased in having made the effort. Taking a longer way home than usual, he detoured through the park and looked out over the pond. A group of men by the chestnut tree gave no interest to him, and he focused instead on the laughing ducks that drifted towards him. Pulling a bag from his pocket he broke up the slice of leftover toast, and threw it in piece by piece. Brian took care to feed each individual bird with a similar amount, but, as always, one large creature shoved the others and snatched more than its share. After casting all of the scraps into the black water, he set towards home. The blackbirds had finished chipping away the morning and now the sparrows churned along the hedge that wrapped the corner, entertaining him as he passed. They seemed to be enjoying themselves as much as he was in the watered down sun. Morning was by far his preferred time of day and he liked to watch the small birds. Sparrows were his favourites.

Brought down onto the pavement by a single swipe, Boris bit into the small pulsing body. He found the dark taste was just as he

45

remembered, slightly sweet, metallic, and beautifully rich. With life draining away, the sparrow could no longer feel the cat's sharp white fangs through its flesh. Tiny barbules from the fine brown feathers began to irritate the cat's throat, causing him to retract his teeth from the bird. He panicked for a second, feeling he might choke. A gritty rasp of a cough freed his airway. Hunting was far too much trouble.

Clair was hurting, and it seemed that no antidote to the tragedy and grief that pressed upon her was to be found. A solitary magpie picked at the roadside and she wished for another to arrive, to change the symbol from one of sorrow to one of joy.

Wanting home, she marched quickly, until her pace was interrupted by an A-board that stuck out into the pavement far enough almost to trip her.

'Art Gallery. Free Entry'

If nothing else, it would be respite from the cold. She took on the grand stone steps just like she would any staircase, and pushed open the door. The whiteness that met her was so removed from her own daily existence that it took a little while for her to adjust. Claire wondered if dying might be similar to entering an art gallery.

Immediately on her left she was met with a large composition of grey angles and heavy lines simply called 'Field'. It didn't look like a field, she thought, and moved along from it in a matter of seconds. Subsequent paintings with names like 'View over the Quay' and 'Garden, July 1952' were just as flippant, and she was relieved to find in the next space a succession of portraits. A straight-faced invigilator sat quietly and leafed through a paperback book, whilst guarding the walls of crooked bodies and faces. Occasionally, the invigilator's eyes glanced up to the others.

The portraits were absorbing, but Clair trusted them less than photographs. She knew that the painted eyes could have been dreamed or imagined, and sometimes the marks on the canvas were barely recognisable as being human at all. As she scanned the walls, each picture bled into the next, some contradicting, and others complimenting, though none made to be together. Quiet on the outside, noisily she began to create theories in her mind as she viewed landscapes bolted to the walls with no option for growth, portraits that rarely looked near human, and the occasional plinth, which housed a tactile bronze beneath a Perspex lid. These Clair longed to touch, to know their cold shapes. As hard as she tried to imagine the metal and echoing the hands of the maker, the distance prevented satisfaction and she returned to the images on the walls.

She was about to leave when she met a scene that seemed to echo her experience more effectively than any photograph she had ever seen.

Every person she had ever met or known was present within it. Figures in a crowd who merged into one another, her parents, Brian, everyone was in those faces with their overlapping emotions. The 1950s vision of a crowd stayed with her even as she re-entered the street. She felt changed.

A silky feather crisscrossed the air, and landed near her feet. She looked upwards but could not see any life at all and wondered if it had been clipped from an angel rather than falling from a migrating goose. Her anxiety had eased since the gallery, and with the appearance of this gentle buffer, she felt even more hopeful. For the first time that day, Clair took out the small pocket camera that lived inside her coat. She framed the feather on the dark ground, isolating it from everything that surrounded it.

Bending to pick up the yellow-topped bottle of milk left on the step in his absence, Brian grimaced at the poor half-eaten sparrow. He strode over it to take in the bottle, put down his keys, and fetch a piece of thick card from inside the hall, which he nauseously shuffled under the bird's body. Acid rose in his throat as the headless creature rolled stiffly onto the card. Absorbed with guilt at having not fed Boris, he flipped the corpse unceremoniously

through the air towards the flowerbed where it landed on a layer of wet leaves.

'Hello again!' came the familiar voice.

Clair had been remembered! As if she had been administered with a small shot of confidence, Clair returned to the shelves and browsed the multitude of sweets.

Swallowing deeply, she summoned a meek 'hello' in return.

'Are you looking for anything particular?' The man asked.

'Um. No. Thank you,' she said, a flush of pink covering her cheeks. *'Where are the mints please'* had failed to find its way out of her mouth.

She wanted to dash out of the door that moment and dodge any further conversation, but tensed her hands into fists inside her pockets and told herself in no uncertain terms to get on with being sociable.

'Are you all right?', he asked with kind intention.

This only made Clair feel worse as she realised she was *visibly* uncomfortable. 'You've read your paper already, have you?' he continued.

Since looking at the paintings and photographing the feather Clair had forgotten all about the newspaper, but her memory jumped

on it again the moment she was asked. Before she could respond he added, 'it's all so sad at the moment, isn't it?'

It seemed he had read her mind. She smiled and nodded. The man turned as a sore voice shouted from a distant room.

'I won't be a minute,' he shouted back, then turned to Clair. 'I've just got to go and see to my Dad. You wouldn't mind keeping an eye on the shop for me, would you?'

He slipped away. Respectfully, she waited, and was hugely relieved when, just two minutes later, the man re-emerged. He thanked her and she felt unusually useful and needed.

'Dad just wanted his water jug filling up. He's not well, you see.'

She was taken aback that a man she had known for a matter of minutes had made such a sudden and personal revelation, and thought carefully before uttering a response. She knew that 'sorry' was the appropriate thing to say, but also that it was helpless and didn't offer very much. Still, he smiled when she said it, though

what he really wanted to do was cry.

'That's him last summer' he said, pointing to a large framed photograph on the wall. In it, a man in a checked shirt was standing proudly beside a garden full of flowers. 'He was fine, then. He loved his garden. Then he got ill. So quick.'

'I'm sorry' Clair said again, struggling for any other words.

'It's alright,' he whispered. 'Happens to us all in the end. We've just got to get on with it, haven't we?' He adjusted the picture frame. 'Make the most of things,' he continued, finely tweaking it, 'show people we care.'

Another customer entered the shop and the man returned to the role of smiling shopkeeper. Clair suddenly thought about Brian. She stepped back into the street and took the direction of home.

Passing the gloved railings, a dark speck came into view and grew in a second to the size of a squash ball. It stopped just inches from Clair's arm. She held still, tried not to rustle in her coat and took a sharp intake of breath as a tiny wren looked at her closely. A speck of sunlight pricked its chest and Clair wondered how small was the heart that beat beneath its feathers. Then, just as quickly as it had appeared, it whirred away into the hedge. She suspected it too had probably taken a sharp breath, frightened by her giant form, but the fleeting moment of closeness with the tiny bird had stopped her heart for a second. She would never forget it.

The death of the tiny sparrow had been brutal and Brian had struggled to forget its headless body lying among the roots. He daren't imagine what its dying moments must have been like. Feeling rather low he decided to make a special meal for the evening to cheer himself.

The garish refrigerator light made everything inside look bland and inedible, but he settled on some pimpled chicken thighs that he put it on the chopping board before withdrawing a sharp knife from the block.

It had been such a jumbled day, and Claire entered home with equally jumbled thoughts. Hanging up her coat, she thought for the first time about what would happen to all the things she owned when she was no longer alive. She had no one to pass them to, and would hate to think of it all being tipped, load-by-load, into a skip. The dresser, the fireplace, the table, the shelves, every surface brimmed with objects. Some meant quite a lot to her, and some she had not really *seen* for years; things that had become a part of her environment to the point of being invisible. She really didn't *need* a wooden antelope with a snapped horn, or a set of brass elephants. She never read any of the books from the top two shelves, and had no interest in playing dominoes, backgammon or cards. Most of her possessions had been inherited from her parents and some of it had stayed in situ, placed by her parents' hands. For the first time, Clair saw that everything was covered in a thick layer of dust, and was swept by a drive to sort out the house, beginning with the dining room.

The ornaments all looked at her blankly, as if they couldn't care less whether they were to stay or go. She took a large brown box from the corner of the room and removed a collection of smaller empty boxes from inside it, then picked up the antelope and ran a hand across its back. A thick cluster of dust drifted to the floor. She hadn't handled the figure for a long time, and could remember her mother giving strict instruction not to touch it. Clair pressed the sharp end of the broken horn with her fingertip. The spike dented her skin and she could almost re-feel the severe punishment from her father. Quickly, she placed the antelope into the box where it faced the side, damaged and shameful.

The place in which the antelope had stood was now a dust-free oval and the empty space left her unsure as to how she might feel in days to come. As a measure of self-protection she began again with the slow ritual of documentation with her camera.

Half an hour before dinner, Brian finished the album, attaching what he believed to be the most recent photograph to the final page. It was a square washed-out snap of a young Clair and her Dad and was the only image in which he really recognised his neighbour. It seemed most apt to be rounding off the story with it. Pleased with himself, he was determined to show Clair the finished book, with hope that it may spark a little respect for her family history again.

The lamp had a long flexible neck that had moved wherever her father had forced it. Clair grabbed it in her hand as if she were to strangle it and turned it towards the bookshelves. The bones in her neck cracked as she bent to read the crawling titles. None were of any interest, and some were completely illegible in broken gold and faded black. She picked out a thick book with a missing spine and inched it from the shelf, taking care not to dislodge the others. The scent of forty years of readers wafted out of the hard green cover, each turn of the stiff pages revealing a thickly printed set of diagrams instructing how to make things. A wooden train, a sailing boat, a garden windmill. Clair had never known her father to make such projects and wondered why it had remained on the shelf at all. She flicked through the project ideas for young men of the time and thought how nice it would have been to have had a different Dad, one who had loved her.

The page 'How to build a pinhole camera' brought happy recollections of the day she was shown how to make photographs with a simple wooden box, but even this was something not learned from her own father, nor from the book in her hands.

She turned the page. Unexpectedly, she was faced with an envelope; unmarked, sealed, and of a quality difficult not to take seriously. Of all the books she could have picked to look at, she felt

sick at having chosen one with a secret. There were too many mysteries now unfolding and she felt annoyed with her father and mother for leaving so many sharp fragments to catch her.

'Read it. What's up with you?' she goaded herself, but the ringing telephone caused her to close the book and put it back. Brian's voice filled her ear.

'Miss Bodmin. I'd like to invite you over to my house. To dinner, 'said Brian pointedly. 'Nothing fancy, and it's not dinner in *that* sense, it's just that there are a few things I wanted to discuss with you and over food seemed like a good way of doing it ...'

With hardly a pause, he continued '... it will only be casserole. I had far too much chicken just for myself and it's too good for the cat. He expects it now you see, and he's already too fat ...'

Without taking any time to think or question, Clair jumped to accept.

'Tomorrow then. About six?' He replied with a disbelieving tone having fully expected her to decline.

As soon as the appointment was made and the brief conversation closed, Clair's face stretched into a worried scowl and she stared at the silent telephone wondering what on earth she had done. Photographs and letters were enough of a problem already,

but now she had made the impulsive decision to go to dinner and she really didn't want to, not at all. Clair didn't *do* dinner with other people.

Everything was spiralling out of control.

Warm hands scraped through the back of Brian's washed hair, making him feel extremely uncomfortable.

'You want the works, eh? Yes, sir. You need it. The whole thing. It's been too long for you.'

Brian didn't like 'the works' as he recalled that it involved not only a haircut but flames inside his ears, scissors up his nostrils, scorching towels and a blade for a razor. The disapproving look he had received from the receptionist on the way in confirmed that it probably *had* been too long and, reluctantly, he agreed. Cold scissors skipped across his neck, and the inevitable questions were fired.

'Going somewhere special tonight, eh? Got a lady friend, eh?'

'No.'

Brian deflected both questions, and also blew a large black fly away as it neared his lip, forcing it into the gaping space of the shop. The barber didn't seem bothered by his one-word response, quite the opposite; he seized the opportunity to launch into a monologue. The occasional word prodded him, but he wasn't really listening. He found more interest in the fly as it flit along the rows of red backed

seats and landed on one customer after another, causing them all to move or scratch. The fly eventually settled next to a hairbrush on the small shelf in front of Brian. It crawled a few paces before rubbing its long front legs together deviously, then proceeded to rub them all the way over its brown head as if also neatening itself up, before lifting off. How entertaining, Brian thought, interrupting people all day, making them itch, changing their position.

He faced the mirror, and watched dead wet hair drop to the floor.

The sun was low when Brian returned home, and Clair's house appeared void of life. He wondered where she was and began to doubt her attendance for dinner. When she knocked at the door a little late Brian was pleased his guest had decided to come at all. The casserole was bubbling and the table was neatly set; he had even wedged a towel in the cat flap to stop Boris from dropping in and out at his leisure.

'You've had your hair cut!' Clair commented. 'It looks very smart!'

Brian had never seen Clair looking so well dressed, either, even though on he outside she still wore the same old coat, which he politely took from her. Making sure she was comfortably seated in the dining room, he went away to dish out the plates of hot food.

In his absence, Clair's vision travelled the walls and surfaces, seeking clues to who Brian was, what he liked, and what he did in this orderly house besides keeping it so clean and tidy. She noticed a collection of photographs boxed closely into frames on the dresser. Each of the frames was of a different style and she wondered if there were any relevance to the faces they contained. Other objects placed about the room seemed mismatched, not as she had expected from her impressions of the man; a carved wood box with a key, a fine china figurine of a young girl with a cat, a tall glass vase with a dense cluster of blooms into it, and a thick green book laid on its side, which she longed to open.

As Clair waited, she wondered why she had been invited for six o'clock. She had normally eaten by five, and the smell of the food drifting through the house was causing irritation to set in. To avert it, she took the risk of leaving the table to view the portraits more closely. Those of Brian reported him as being happy- sitting behind a desk, wearing a prize rosette for something, and standing with a reflective expression on a small wooden bridge in what appeared to be a tropical greenhouse. He was instantly recognisable in all of them, but the photograph on the bridge seemed to capture him most closely and she peered closely at it. His eyes seemed to sparkle and his face glowed with life; she could not fail to be impressed both by his radiance and by the skill of the photographer. The other photographs were of people she could only guess about, whom she

might find the courage to ask about during dinner. Then she noticed, tucked among the adult faces, a tiny silver frame. No more than two inches high, contained with in it was a photograph of a very young child. Boy or girl she could not tell as the downy hair and yellow suit did not reveal a gender. She reached to pick it up and, as she did, caught the flowers with her arm. The round vase rocked over onto the dresser top, and, to Clair's relief, not only had it fallen into a gap avoiding the other picture frames, but the incident had happened just as something clattered loudly in the kitchen.

Nervously, she righted the vase. The flower stems were so tightly packed that none had come out and, squashing them to one side, she held the vase just under the lip of the dresser top to channel the small puddle of spilled water back into the neck with her hand. After several attempts, she acknowledged the impossibility of the task and wiped the dresser instead with the sleeve of her jumper. A fine run or two of water had trickled down to the carpet, landing amid the dark pattern that, thankfully, made the patch unnoticeable. Before returning to her seat, she checked the vase one more time. The ruffled pink heads were a little crooked but, buttoned shut, they would not share this secret.

'Nothing ever goes back to how it was,' she sighed.

Without touching another thing, she took her place back at the table just as Brian appeared in the doorway carrying two plates.

'Sorry it took so long,' he apologised. 'I hope you weren't bored.'

Boris pushed several times at the flap that was his usual means of entry but it wouldn't budge. He flicked his tail from side to side.

He had plenty of other houses to go in.

Clair looked at Brian. She noted how his hair shone and his thin fingers whitened as they pressed on his fork. His wrists were thin, too, and his chain-like watchstrap rocked back and forth as he sliced the chicken into small morsels on his plate. Too shy to watch him put the fork all the way to his mouth, she scanned the room whenever he lifted it, and checked the dresser once or twice.

The large green book lay sleeping; she wondered what could be inside it; whether it was ever disturbed. There was no dust on it, but there didn't seem to be dust anywhere. Her eyes skipped as she looked now for dust, comparing Brian's neatness with the blurred coating inside her own house. She was pleased when she spotted some; a tiny furred line along the bevelled edge of a mirror.

Concerned by Clair's distractedness, Brian stopped chewing. 'Is everything all right?' he asked, and poured two glasses of wine from a thick green bottle.

'It's very good. Thank you.'

Brian began gathering vegetables, taking care to avoid the shoulder-wrenching squeak that sometimes happens when a fork meets a plate, and they ate mostly in quietness, enjoying being in the same room and savouring the taste of day-old stew. Whenever glances met, the gaze was uncomfortable and diverted. When Brian did find a moment to examine Clair's face more carefully, he saw she was looking in the direction of the green book.

'Would you like to see it?' he asked excitedly. He had been hoping she would ask. She was about to say 'yes' when he continued, 'it's a photograph album. I think you'll like it. You might even recognise one or two ...'

Clair hesitated, realising that it was probably *the* photographs, *her* photographs.

'No. Thank you.' She replied.

The corners of Brian's mouth dropped some way between sadness and annoyance, but he put his knife and fork neatly together

and picked up the bottle from the centre of the table.

'More wine?' He invited, masking his disappointment with politeness.

Not waiting for an answer, he leaned across and the yellow wine glugged into her glass.

'Thank you.' she said again, then, remembering the reason for her visit, changed the subject.

'By the way, I wanted to tell you that the tree is being cut in the morning.'

'Oh that's wonderful Miss Bodmin! Cut down? Thank you! It'll be so much better without the dark shadow of it. And without those noisy birds.'

Clair didn't find the confidence to tell him that it was only being lopped, but following his delight she wondered whether she should ring the tree surgeon and increase the order to a full felling. The combination of good news and good wine unlocked Brian and he proceeded to tell her about the various ways his tree-less life would improve. He also told her excitedly about the previous day's incident.

'Did I tell you Boris caught a sparrow? Wicked cat. Its head was right off, poor thing. Nothing there, just feathers and a little dead body. I was very sad about it. I do like sparrows.'

Clair lay down her knife and fork. Her thoughts turned to the doves; she would miss them when the tree was gone.

'The food was lovely, Brian. You are a very good cook.' She complimented, despite having left a rather large portion.

'Thank you, Miss Bodmin. I am glad you liked it.' He blushed a little, forgetting to tell her the rest of his news.

The second he heard the fork ringing against the side of his earthenware bowl Boris rushed towards the house and darted for the door. The flap was now open and he leapt through in anticipation of a hearty meal. He was not disappointed.

Warmth and satisfaction hadn't lasted very long at all. Clair had enjoyed the dinner but had also anticipated her own downheartedness before it flooded her. She turned the key and stepped into her cold, empty space. She thought about getting some flowers for the dresser, to cheer the place up and make it homely, like

Brian's, but as she flicked on the light the idea was quickly dismissed; a new vase would become just another collector of dust.

That night, Clair's thoughts wouldn't seem to rest on one subject and ideas tumbled about haphazardly as she tried to sleep: the tree; the house; the book; the envelope; her parents; the birds; everything. The random imaginations seemed to narrow and fall like sand in an hourglass. As they dropped away everything and everyone was filtered out. Everyone except Brian. She joined her hands under the back of her head and lay awake. She saw a figure walking around her house, filling the kettle in her kitchen, sitting at her dining table, snipping bunches of grapes into her fruit bowl. Maddeningly, no matter how hard she tried to see *him*, she failed. Brian's face was never present and she couldn't identify her imaginary cohabitant at all. As the night ticked on, coldness gripped the room causing her breath to leave her body in a visible funnel. She pulled the heavy blankets tightly around her feeling their woolen load against her skin. A high-pitched bark pierced the night having found its way in through several gaps in the window frames. Clair envisioned a small dog, hungry to its core, ignored by everyone. She imagined the poor creature had nowhere to curl up and could only pace in circles stopping to bid for attention. Clair thought how fortunate she was to have a bed and a roof, and felt glad that she had not come into this world as a dog. The dog's cries accompanied her as she fell into a sleep. Outside, tiny flows of rainwater ran musically between the cobbles and she was lured into a dream.

...

Lying on one side the dog stretched out long, thin legs. Then, like a frame from Muybridge the dog lay still, except for her ribs rising up and down and her heart thumping visibly beneath an inadequate layer of hair. From time to time one watery brown eye opened and her nose twitched. Clair wanted nothing more than to protect her from harm but in all directions, translucent red walls reflected in multiple directions making it difficult to know exactly where the dog was lying. Her half black, half white body appeared in different degrees of opacity, and her legs pointed at different angles. Clair couldn't seem to attract her attention through sound or motion. Unable to calculate where the real dog lay, she knew she would have to go in and search. Among the maze of thin, mirror-like screens, she felt panicked. There was little time, and the grey strangers drifting past didn't seem aware of her escalating distress. Clair tried to shout but her words formed nothing more than a gurgle.

She felt the trail of a helpless tear down the length of her cheek. The grey ceiling seemed closer than normal and beside her the clock glowed 2.22. There was something about 2.22; it prodded her awake most nights, usually without a dream in her head. This time, with a wet face and pillow, she knew she had been crying and remembered the dog, trapped and alone in the kaleidoscope place.

Sick with tiredness, she watched the shadows in the room float into a multitude of shapes before sobbing back into the darkness.

The sky was without a single star. Brian pulled the cloud-soft quilt around his face and under his chin. His closed eyes brought a passing picture of Clair before the hazy vision became the face of her father. Tired and needing rest in advance of a very busy day, he slipped further down into the bed and tried to clear everything from his mind. As the tangible world gradually faded, Brian wondered whether he was too stuffy, too *severe*. Perhaps time alone had led him to become obsessive about things that weren't important at all. As the night stepped up, he made the decision that, tomorrow, he would begin to live more freely.

Boris had carved a warm, deep circle in the ridge created by Brian's knees. It accommodated his curled body perfectly. In the darkness, and feeling safe from the dangers of the outside, he thought only of food.

Everywhere in his sleep were sparrows. All he had to do was reach out and grab them and they were his.

Outside, slow and sturdy in the wintry air, the tree sheltered the resting birds. With their heads beneath their wings, the cold barely disturbed them. Predatory night birds took short rests at the very top of the tree as they scrutinised the ground for small mammals to carry away.

The tiniest creatures continued with their labour. Moving quickly, they had much work still to do.

A coppery glow, so deep it seemed to have no end, was Clair's first experience of the new day. Conscious, she chose not to open her eyes and, instead, sunk into the colour, travelling and enjoying its depth as much as the night sky. As she proceeded into the endless field, tiny spangles and faces-in-negative came to her, forming and melting so quickly that she could not fix on any one of them for long enough to see who or what they were. It was enthralling, and, half awake, she stayed to watch the changing shapes. Perhaps it was the blood passing around her eyes, glowing orange against the presumptuous sunlight, but that didn't explain the shapes. She saw her mother smiling, and wanted to hold it there, but just as quickly as she had thought it, the face had gone again, transformed into something else. Disappointment opened up her eyes. Already feeling bereft, she heard the first swaying branch as it

snapped and hung like a broken arm before cracking onto the pavement. She had forgotten it was the day of the tree work and could not help herself from looking out just as the chainsaw sliced into the trunk of the tree.

By the time Clair was dressed there was nothing left but an orange stump and a pile of vivid sawdust as the bleeding remnants of the tree were loaded onto a trailer and taken away.

The tree pushed sap out into the air in an attempt to repair itself and prevent any infection from getting in. It knew only to pump the soothing fluid around its frame.

A solitary dove garbled onto the dying stump and strutted around it.

Tilting its head from side to it waited patiently for the tree to come back.

For the first time Brian could see the entire front of Clair's house, and a small glimpse of the hill beyond that had been hidden from him for years. The whole place seemed much lighter and he

was delighted; if not for himself then for whoever else might step into his house.

'About time,' was all he could say, and planned to thank Clair later, as well as giving her the photo album, which waited, in a box by the front door.

Brian had such a lot to do that day, but before his typewriter was packed away, he sat at the desk to begin composing a round-robin letter, updating his relatives on all the goings-on. He clattered out words about the tree, the cat, the street, his neighbour, and when he had finished typing, he slipped on some boots and his thickest coat and stepped outside.

Small remains of sawdust and greenery littered the street, not yet carried by the winter wind. Brian found Clair already in her front garden, oblivious to the cold, staring at the tree stump.

'I see you have done it! Well done, Miss Bodmin. Very community spirited of you.' Brian declared.
'Would you like to come in?' She asked, with loss in her voice.

'No, thank you. I just have a small favour to ask.'

'Do you want me to knock the wall down for you?' She replied with a hint of cynicism.

'Not at all! The wall is fine.' He replied. 'Actually I was coming to ask you about photographs.'

'I'm not burning any today, if that's what you want to know.'

'Miss Bodmin, I can tell this isn't a good time. Shall I come back?'

'Sorry.' She raised her tone and tried to sound less upset. 'What can I do for you, Brian?'

As she spoke, she tried to focus attention on him and not on the stub of the tree, but it was too difficult to take her eyes from it. Nothing looked right anymore; the garden, the houses, the sky. She dreaded any stupid idea that Brian might come out with next.

'I was thinking,' he began, but paused as she noticed Clair's expression turn to mistrust. 'I was thinking,' he repeated, 'about you being a photographer.' Her eyebrows raised with interest this time. 'I wondered if you might take my photograph? A proper one, one I can send to my family. A portrait for Christmas.'

Clair felt flattered that he had remembered this detail, having told Brian in passing that she had *been* a photographer. In some ways she supposed she still was.

'Why not?' she replied. 'Shall we do it tomorrow? Why don't you wear your blue shirt again?'

'All right', he agreed, with a slight blush.

The moment he had suggested it, Clair was already visualising the image she wanted to create. Relieved by this unexpected distraction, she went inside to prepare her camera.

In a flash, Boris leapt out of the chair and landed in the small rectangle of pale sunlight that had appeared on the carpet. He enjoyed the minor increase in warmth and was pleased with himself for having made the decision to jump.

The following day prompted nausea as Clair delayed getting up out of bed and getting ready for the first portrait shoot she had worked on in years. She tried to validate her sickness as being anything but nervousness about the day ahead, but her stomach turned itself over and over as always when she was about to do something outside of the house. A flood of flaky excuses sprang to mind.

She rolled onto her back and stared blankly upwards, until a spider caught her attention. It manoeuvred clumsily along the jagged surface and she wondered if it had any idea where it was going. She tried to predict its route but could not guess the spider's next move as it changed direction again and again, directly above her, and Clair became unnerved as to whether it might fall off. Watching the tiny creature blunder along stirred her to confront her own direction. With an overwhelming wash of fear, she realised that she was completely alone with no other living being to share her ideas, or her life. Colour left her flesh as she swallowed hard and watched the creature stumble to the edge of the wall. After years of bumbling along by herself, the black hole of loneliness had finally opened underneath her.

Tired of tackling the difficult terrain, the spider chose to descend on a line so thin that it belied any effort. As his cold body abseiled in stages he lost strength with every inch of the drop. He did not know at all where he would land or what he would find, but the spider didn't know anxiety; from experience it knew it would find the ground.

That was knowledge enough.

Clair's self absorption could easily have swamped her, sucked her in to days and days of brutal rumination, but instead, with an unusual energy she jumped from her bed.

Bracing her pale body, she breathed cold air hard into her lungs and shook out her arms until the tension in her shoulders loosened. Invisible tears still gathered in bags beneath her eyes and her stomach still shook, but despite all her sadness and fear, only she could change things, and there was no time like the present.

Brian stood in his dressing gown, wondering which outfit to wear for the photo shoot. Like thin shadows, his clothes draped in sets over the neatly made bed; a grey suit, a black shirt with a poppy red tie, and three slightly different ensembles of blue. He had favourite combinations, but Clair's comment about the blue was rattling his decision-making. It was not long before she was due to arrive, and though uncertain whether she would, he settled on his clothes.

With shaking hands, Clair clutched the camera bag. From her raised position on the steps, she could see a small view of a distant

landscape that she had never seen before and promised she would go there, one day.

'Hello!' Brian ushered her in and closed the door. 'I see you have your camera! Good!' She could tell he was excited. 'Where shall we go? In here?' He opened up the door to the sunny front room.

Clair, unclipped her bag and cleaned and adjusted her camera. As she adjusted the settings Brian pulled out a dining chair and sat down, moving to find a position that was comfortable.

'Am I OK here?' he asked. She couldn't help but take a shot as he spoke. 'That's great. Don't move.' He held still, looking into the camera without a blink. 'Now turn your head a little, towards the window. That's it. Hold it there.' She moved

around   him,   changing   angles   and   settings.

Relaxed, Brian naturalised his smile. Clair smiled too, behind the camera. She could smell his freshly laundered shirt and see the neat line across where his hair had been cut. Brian was surprised at his comfort with both Clair and the camera; he found he rather liked the attention. For Clair, it was the closest she had felt to anyone for a long time.

The 36th frame was sure to be the best, she thought, as by the end of the roll her subject was perfectly relaxed.

'Thank you Clair, I am sure you have done a good job' said Brian.

She was about to load another film, to do it all again, but he stood up and asked if she would like a cup of tea.

'Just a drop of milk for me.' she said, and put the camera back into the bag, closing it into the darkness.

'When will I see the prints?' he shouted from the kitchen.

'A few days.' she shouted back. 'I'll bring them across.'

'Don't worry. If you could give me the film I'll sort it. I might not have time to wait.'

'Are you sure?'

'Positive!'

When Brian returned he carried two large china mugs of tea and placed hers carefully onto the table beside her.

'Here you are! You've earned it.'

She placed the spent film on the table next to him. 'Thank you.' She said. 'So have you.'

Simultaneously, they picked up their cups and blew gently before sipping, quietly keeping their greater thoughts to themselves.

A loud cough echoed around the houses as the man in brown stood on the steps outside Brian's. He continued biting into the floury bread and swallowed the cough along with the warm butter and bacon. With no sign of anyone coming to the door, he finished his breakfast, and pulled a mobile phone from his pocket to check the time. He was early, but that was better than being late given the amount of work there was to do.

In his dressing gown, Brian opened the door. 'Can you give me half an hour?' he asked, his voice as cold as the November air.

The only parts of Clair visible amongst the heap of blankets were her mouth and nose, through a small egg-shaped fold. She had tried opening her eyes once but had soon closed them again and pulled the bedding even tighter around her head. She lay snug and still. Eyes closed, she tried to envisage what was to come. There was no major plan today. Eating, washing, reading, photographing, feeding the birds, then sorting through some more books. A warm coloured vision of Brian delayed further the transition from cosy nest to cold room and, even though a distant noise outside annoyed her, she couldn't extract herself from the comfort of the bed.

Lying on her side, curled like a baby, Clair fell asleep again lulled by the sound of her own heartbeat running slowly on.

Palpitating faster than it had ever done before and, unable to see a way out, Boris called repeatedly for assistance. The pungencies of plastic and disinfectant were revolting, but worse was the inability to move inside his constricted enclosure. Turning around was not an option, and the thin blanket that had been placed on the floor provided no relief. Despite increasing distress in his voice, there was no help. The container moved and he slid backwards. He extended his claws to try and hold fast as a swaying motion took over, almost making him sick.

He would never trust a human again.

A loud and unfamiliar noise roused Clair from her bed and she looked out over the street. The man dressed in brown emerged from Brian's house supporting the end of a large, long box, followed by a second man who seemed to be struggling with the other end. Carefully they trod down the steps, shouting instructions as the awkwardness of the box and the steps conspired to get the better of them.

They made their way up a thick wooden ramp into the back of a truck painted with an arc of thick black letters.

'Solus Removals'.

Suddenly Clair didn't want breakfast; she didn't want anything. Not knowing *what* to do, she ran downstairs and flung open the door. Words had dried to the back of her throat preventing her from yelling and even swallowing had become almost impossible. In thin slippers, she set across the road, her dressing gown flapping open, revealing her flannelette pyjamas. The road seemed to be soft as mud, sucking her in and slowing her movements as she tried to run.

'Brian, are you there?' she gasped, as she reached the stone steps.

''Excuse me, Miss' said one of the men. He pushed past, not giving her the space to step aside. She went inside after him.

'Miss Bodmin! What are you doing here? And why on earth are you wearing your dressing gown?' Brian's face was as if he had been witness to a spectre.

'Brian!' Clair grabbed the post at the foot of the staircase and clung onto it. 'There's a removal van outside your house,' she blurted.

Though he tried not to, Brian could not help but laugh.

'Of course there is. I'm moving house today!' His voice echoed around what was now an almost empty space. Clair shook her head, still breathless.

'Here. I have something for you.' He picked up a large green book and held it out to her. 'I kept it for you.'

'I don't want it,' she exclaimed, realising immediately what it was. 'You wanted it. It's yours.' She was rather shocked that he had had enough of it already, and pushed it back.

Like a slide show her mind flicked through the dinner, the photo shoot, the telephone calls. She remembered many exchanges, but regardless how hard she searched she could not pinpoint the words 'I'm moving house' or 'I'm leaving' or anything of the sort in the archive of her mind.

'Are you absolutely sure you don't want it, Miss Bodmin, because I can't keep it any more. I thought you would like it. It's your family. It must mean something to you.'

'Just put it in the bin,' she suggested, 'or the charity shop;' one chain of words she did remember clearly was the string he had used in outrage over her methods for disposing of photographs.

Brian propped the book up on the floor.

'I am sorry Clair, I have a lot to do.' He sauntered away leaving her clinging to the post as if the tide were grasping around her feet.

The following days were grief-filled. Just like her mother and everyone else she had ever cared about, Brian was gone from her life. She looked out over the lifeless windows of his home.

As time stretched and the days became long, she occupied herself by systematically clearing through the shelves of books. Some she placed in piles on the floor in the hallway, and others into boxes. A few stayed on the shelves to be read - one day. In another box she had carefully placed her cameras, and, beside them, paper wallets full of photographs; records of things, events, people; reminders of her traumas. Clearing out the large drawer in the dresser she scooped out all of the unprocessed films and dropped them into the kitchen pedal bin. She had no interest in them any more, and didn't want them to fall into a stranger's hands. There were many more than she had realised; 35mm, 120, even a couple of old 110s.

When everything was ready, she folded closed the box containing her treasured camera and put on her coat. It wasn't too heavy to carry into town, and using her back, Clair pushed open the door of the first charity shop she came to. Faces of children in poverty and sadness covered the walls, and she wondered why she hadn't given her things away sooner. Two assistants were busy at the back of the shop, and she placed the box carefully and discreetly on the floor beside the counter.

The sense of a good deed carried her lightly home and she felt assured that that any money raised would buy a new tap or a supply of medicine for someone, somewhere.

Later that day, as the hunters and dealers flicked through Clair's photographs, they were met with a confusion of history and narrative that would eventually penetrate their own dreams. Some photographs were purchased for aesthetics, some for an interest in specific details, and others for coincidental likenesses. At twenty pence each they sold quickly and were soon scattered over the town and beyond. At least a half a dozen browsers picked up the camera before it was sold. They looked through, examined the lens, operated the shutter, and checked all was well. Eventually, it was placed it on the glass counter-top as the buyer took out his wallet.

'It doesn't matter if it works or not. It'll look great on the shelf,' the buyer explained enthusiastically before dropping it into the bottom of a carrier bag.

'What a good idea' the shop volunteer said and put the money in the till where the clips pinched it fast.

With no clutter, no cameras, no tree and no Brian, Clair's life had quickly changed beyond recognition. She had immersed herself in making the house clean and orderly, and, though there was still a long way to go, she had made progress. Everything was going very

well, until, one day, the letterbox flapped and a thick envelope thudded onto the floor.

Clair rushed to the window in the sitting room and leaned forwards, her nose almost touching the glass. She hadn't heard the loose catch clink on the gate, nor was there anyone in sight. Without too much thought, and telling herself not to be concerned, she picked it up and placed it unopened in a drawer. She didn't plan to open it, not just yet. Her quiet life was rarely interrupted these days, and she seemed to have found a new capacity for coping. Even the sickness had respited.

Then, one afternoon there came a firm knock at the door. New confidence permitted her to open it, and there stood a man much taller than she was, and much older. He had white hair, a thin smile and crinkles at the corners of his eyes. He looked slightly familiar, but Clair could not place him.

'I don't want to buy anything, thank you, and I am not religious, so please go away if you are selling or preaching,' Clair blurted.

The familiarity of the smiling face in front of her was beginning to annoy her.

'Actually, I'm wondering if you can help,' the man said with polite depth.

'Help?' queried Clair. She didn't know yet what the request entailed but had already decided that there was nothing she could possibly do. 'I can't help you.'

'I know this might sound like a strange question,' he continued, 'but have you received anything unusual in the post? Photographs, that sort of thing?'

Clair's expression answered the question wordlessly and anxiety washed through her as she began to recall the entire chain of events from the arrival of the first packet.

'Ah, so you did receive them.' The man deduced.

'Of course I received them, and what a shock it was. I really didn't know what to do.'

'Well, no, I don't suppose you would.' He sounded sympathetic after witnessing her upset.

'Are you his brother or something?' she asked.

'I'm sorry, I don't understand.'

'Well,' she continued, 'Dad's been dead for years.'

'Dad?'

'Yes. Dad. Are you from his sister's side then?'

'I'm not from any side. I'm from Liverpool.'

'Liverpool? Who *are* you? What do you want from *me*? I hope you haven't brought me more photos'

'Quite the opposite, actually. I've come to collect.' He noted her bewilderment and tried to explain. 'The photographs! You see, I made a terrible mistake and I am here to ask for them back.'

Clair's searched, unable to process what she was hearing.

'You don't know me.' The man continued. 'I don't know you either. I just sent them here. To this address. By mistake.'

'But I'm Clair. You know I'm Clair. You wrote my name on them.'

'Oh no.' The man slapped his leather-gloved hand across his open mouth, realising at that moment exactly what had happened. 'I am so sorry. Those photographs weren't for you, they were meant for another Clair, *my* Clair. I'm afraid they were sent to the wrong address, the wrong house. The addresses are similar you see. Clair moved and … Look, I'm truly sorry if it's caused you inconvenience'

The insight was like a kick to her stomach. The photographs were not of her. They were not of her father, either. They were nothing to do with her. She felt suddenly very stupid and her face flushed redder and redder. She had assumed everything.

'So can I have them back please?' asked the man, breaking the silence that had transpired.

'I gave them away. Most of them,' she whispered, to the charity shop in the town. He looked startled. Then she remembered the unopened packet in the drawer. 'Wait there. Are these yours?'

Tears welled up in the man's eyes.

'Yes, they are! Thank you! That's wonderful!' He clasped the packet protectively to his chest and apologised heavily before bidding Clair goodbye and promising there would be no more deliveries. She daren't tell the stranger about the burnings, or the album, and decided it was best to leave it as it was, allowing him some sense of reprieve.

As he left, Clair mumbled to herself how the whole series of events had been stranger than fiction. Perhaps it *had* all been a fiction, she thought.

With only days until Christmas, Brian sat at his new desk to begin addressing envelopes to friends and family.   Turning to *B* in his address book, he saw the name *Clair Bodmin* and wondered whether he should bother to send her a card.   He looked at Boris sleeping in his new corner and though about it.   They had both moved on now and it would mean the cost of another stamp.   But as he lifted the next card from the assorted box, it seemed his mind was made for him.   The image was a tall evergreen tree dotted with falling snow.   Above the tree, a pair of white birds flew in a starry sky and Victorian script leaned the words *'two turtle doves'*.

Brian twisted his pen in his hands wondering how best to write to an ex-neighbour.   He didn't want to say much, just a few quick lines to let Clair know that she hadn't been entirely forgotten, not yet. He looked around the room for inspiration to the smiling portraits of friends, family, and the little yellow-wrapped half sister he had never known.

'Dear Miss Bodmin,
I saw this and thought of you.
Have a happy Christmas.
Brian.'

Aligned with the fold, he carefully placed in a photograph of himself.   Happy and relaxed in his best blue shirt; the 36th frame.

Clair saw a glimpse of red from the postman's coat and she was at the door before he had even entered the gate.

'Miss Bodmin?' he confirmed, and she scribbled a tangled signature. He handed her a packet and a few thin envelopes. As usual, she propped the letters unopened behind the clock, but took the heavy packet into the house and tore it open, releasing from the dull wrapping a length of pale blue-green fabric. It unfurled itself and tumbled like a summer waterfall onto the floor. Clair tracked her palm along it, feeling the smooth, cool material and breathing in the cotton scent. She was delighted; she had never bought curtains before. Satisfied that the contents were correct, she went into the dining room and pulled out a chair, then, kicking away her slippers she stepped up onto it. Methodically, she snapped off the discoloured plastic hooks one by one from the track and the first old orange drape collapsed to the ground in an exhausted heap. The thin winter sun streamed in through ribbons of dust and she squinted to absorb the view, trying not to sneeze. It took a little patience, and made her arms ache, but once the air had cleared and the curtains were in place, the room looked very different; it was much more modern, much more *Clair*. All the surfaces were cleaned and shining with polish with space made for a tiny Christmas tree, Clair's first since she had found herself alone in the world. She glanced over at the letters, but decided she would make some tea before opening

any. Instead she wanted to sit for a while and enjoy the space, *her* space.

Alone but for the voices of two doves echoing down the chimney, she felt ready for her own quiet Christmas and ready for the coming year. She had so many plans. It seemed everything had been painted with a colourful coating and she could not help but smile.

The end.

---

* 'The Little Prince' by Antoine de Saint Exupéry (1943) translated by Ros and Chloe Shwarz (2010)

68

© 2019 J D Dennis

Text and cover image by J D Dennis

First published 2019
All rights reserved

16

Printed in Poland
by Amazon Fulfillment
Poland Sp. z o.o., Wrocław

50945649R00051

RETURN TO the circulation desk of any
University of California Library
or to the

NORTHERN REGIONAL LIBRARY FACILITY
Bldg. 400, Richmond Field Station
University of California
Richmond, CA 94804-4698

ALL BOOKS MAY BE RECALLED AFTER 7 DAYS
2-month loans may be renewed by calling
(510) 642-6753
1-year loans may be recharged by bringing books
to NRLF
Renewals and recharges may be made 4 days
prior to due date

DUE AS STAMPED BELOW

OCT 28 1993

DEC 29 1992

Returned by

NOV 1 6 1992

nta Cruz Jimev

NOV 1 9 1994

DEC 0 6 1996

LD 21A–50m-4,'60
(A9562s10)476B

General Library
University of California
Berkeley